GHOST IN THE GRAND

BY JOHNATHAN RAND

ILLUSTRATIONS BY DARRIN BREGE

Don't miss these exciting books by Johnathan Rand!

Michigan Chillers:

#1: Mayhem on Mackinac Island
#2: Terror Stalks Traverse City
#3: Poltergeists of Petoskey
#4: Aliens Attack Alpena
#5: Gargoyles of Gaylord
#6: Strange Spirits of St. Ignace
#7: Kreepy Klowns of Kalamazoo
#8: Dinosaurs Destroy Detroit
#9: Sinister Spiders of Saginaw
#10: Mackinaw City Mummies

American Chillers:

#1: The Michigan Mega-Monsters
#2: Ogres of Ohio
#3: Florida Fog Phantoms
#4: New York Ninjas
#5: Terrible Tractors of Texas
#6: Invisible Iguanas of Illinois
#7: Wisconsin Werewolves
#8: Minnesota Mall Mannequins
#9: Iron Insects Invade Indiana
#10: Missouri Madhouse
#11: Poisonous Pythons Paralyze Pennsylvania
#12: Dangerous Dolls of Delaware

Adventure Club:

Ghost in the Graveyard

AudioCraft Publishing, Inc.
PO Box 281
Topinabee Island, MI 49791

www.americanchillers.com

An AudioCraft Publishing, Inc. book

This book is a work of fiction. Names, places, characters and incidents are used fictitiously, or are products of the author's very active imagination.

Graphics layout/design consultant: Scott Beard, Straits Area Printing
Honorary graphics consultant: Chuck Beard *(we miss you, Chuck)*
Editors: Diane Gurnee, Kristen Kelley, Carly Pitrago, Sheri Kelley

Book warehouse and storage facilities provided by Clarence and Dorienne's Storage, Car Rental & Shuttle Service, Topinabee Island, MI

Warehouse security provided by Salty, Abby, & Lily Munster.

paperback edition ISBN 1-893699-62-5
hardcover edition ISBN 1-893699-61-7

Printed in USA

First Printing - January, 2004

Also by Johnathan Rand:

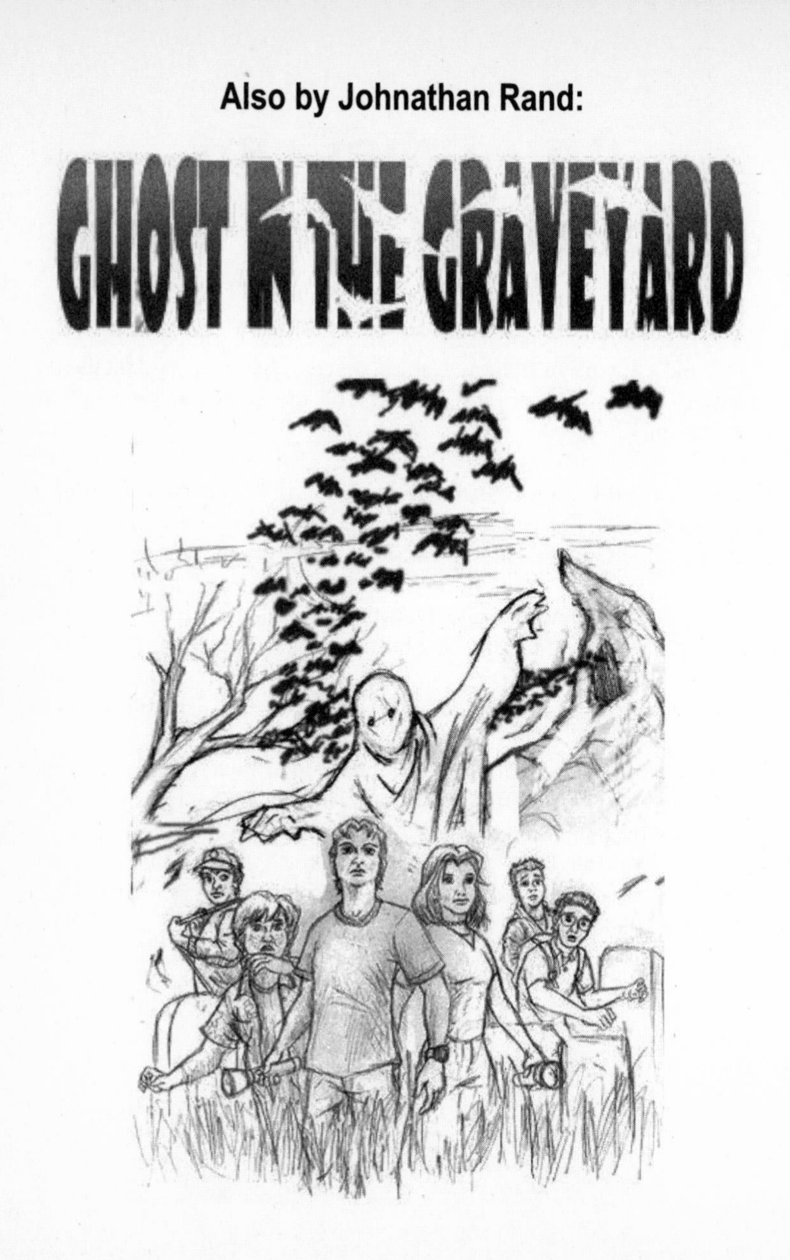

Table of Contents

1. The Great Treasure Hunt	9
2. Clubhouse Catastrophe	97
3. Raising the Independence	141
4. Ghost in the Grand	221
5. Firestorm	281
6. The Secret of the Ancient Totem	339

THE GREAT TREASURE HUNT

1

In the town of Great Bear Heart, there's an old story that goes like this:

Sometime in the 1920's, three men robbed a bank in Detroit. To get away from the police, who were in hot pursuit, they hopped a train and rode it all the way to our little town on the shores of Puckett Lake. They hid out in a tunnel in the ground below the old railroad depot—what is now the Great Bear Heart Library.

They were soon discovered by the local police, but the robbers took off and hid in a small house nearby. There was a shoot-out and the robbers were killed, but the stolen loot—which happened to be a bag of silver dollars—was never found.

Ever since, there's been a lot of speculation as to

what happened to the money. Some say that the robbers buried it in the forest. Still other people believe that it was found by someone shortly after the robbers died, and whoever found the stolen loot didn't turn it in to the police.

Club member Dylan Bunker found an old silver dollar—a 'Peace Dollar'— in the tunnel one day. Peace Dollars were made shortly after World War One, and they were made of pure silver. On one side of the coin is the liberty head, and on the other is an eagle holding a laurel wreath. Today, each coin, in good condition, is worth about twenty dollars.

We were certain that the coin Dylan found must be part of the bank robbers' loot. The six of us in the Adventure Club—Shane Mitchell, Holly O'Mara, Lyle Haywood, Tony Gritter, Dylan Bunker and myself—searched and searched, but we didn't find any more silver dollars.

All of that changed one rainy Saturday morning.

Holly O'Mara and I were supposed to go for a bike ride, but the rain postponed our plans. Instead, we decided to play checkers over at her house.

I put on my raincoat and boots and began the short walk to Holly's house. The morning was gray, and rain fell straight down in a heavy drizzle. Rivers of water slithered over the paved road. I watched a leaf float by like a tiny sailboat. It spun and swirled as it bobbed along, swept by the speeding current of the small rivulet. It had been raining for nearly two days straight, but it was supposed to end by late afternoon.

I was only a block from Holly's house when I caught a movement of something small out of the corner of my eye. I turned to see a kitten, its gray fur completely soaked, staring back at me from the open door of an abandoned shed.

I stopped walking. *"Hey Buddy,"* I called out to the tiny creature. I took a step toward it, and the animal immediately disappeared into the shed.

Poor thing, I thought. *Stuck out in the rain like that. Hope he has a home.*

When I got to Holly's house and told her about the kitten I had spotted, her eyes got huge.

"We have to help him!" she exclaimed.

"I tried to get close, but it ran and hid," I replied.

"We have to find him," Holly said urgently. "We have to find him and help him!"

When Holly makes up her mind about something, there's not much use in trying to change it. And when it comes to animals, she has a soft spot the size of a basketball. She can't stand to see an animal in trouble.

Holly didn't have a raincoat, but she had a big umbrella that was big enough for both of us. The rain was coming down heavier now, and it beat the umbrella like a drum as we hustled down the rain-gorged street.

"Where did you see him?" Holly asked.

"Right over there," I pointed. "He was sitting in the doorway of that old shed."

"What kind of cat was it?" she asked.

I shrugged. "I don't know," I replied. "It was a gray cat. And it was soaked."

"It's probably starving," Holly said.

We cut across the wet grass and walked over to the shed. My eyes darted around, searching for the drenched kitten.

Which, of course, we would find.

But it wasn't the only thing we would discover in the shed. What we were about to find in the shed was going to send Holly and me—and everyone else in the Adventure Club—on one of the wildest goose chases of the summer.

2

We were almost to the open doorway. Through the downpour, we could see piles of old boxes and broken chairs inside. Suddenly, Holly spotted the tiny creature huddled at the back of the shed. Her hand shot out, pointing.

"There he is!"

The kitten was sitting on a piece of wood. The creature was completely soaked, like it had been swimming. Its fur was matted together, heavy with water. Huge, fearful eyes stared back at us. The tiny animal trembled, perhaps because it was cold, or maybe because it was afraid of the two figures that suddenly appeared in the doorway of the shed.

"Oh, the poor thing!" Holly exclaimed. She knelt down in the door of the shed and reached out her hand. "Come here," she coaxed sweetly. "We're not going to hurt you."

The kitten remained where it was, sitting on the piece of wood. It wasn't going *anywhere.* I think it was too afraid.

"Help me move some of this stuff out of the way," Holly said. She stood up slowly, and the kitten craned its neck back, watching cautiously.

"We're going to scare him off," I warned.

"Just move slow," Holly replied. "He's really frightened."

Carefully, we lifted some of the old crates and debris out of our way. The cat really couldn't go anywhere except out the front door of the shed, so it would have to get past us first. At the moment, it didn't look too anxious to go anywhere.

We piled the stuff off to the side. Mostly, the shed was filled with old crates and wooden boxes. All of them were empty, and some of them fell apart in our hands. One box crumbled the moment I picked it up, and pieces fell to the floor. The crash spooked the kitten, and it huddled even further into the corner of the shed, trembling in fear.

"You scared him!" Holly scolded.

I shrugged in defense. "I didn't do it on purpose," I replied.

Slowly, Holly made her way closer to the cat. When she was only a few feet away, she bent down and extended her hand.

"Come on, little guy," she urged. "Nobody is going to hurt you. Come on."

The cat remained where it was, huddled in the corner of the shed. Thunder boomed, shaking the old structure and sending a wave of horror through the kitten.

And for whatever reason, the creature must have decided that Holly wasn't going to hurt it after all, because it cautiously stepped from the piece of wood and slunk warily to Holly's outstretched hand. It stretched its neck up until its head touched her fingers.

Holly scratched behind the kitten's ears. "There, there," she said softly. "See? We're not going to hurt you."

The kitten responded by arching its back and rubbing its nose on Holly's hand.

"I think he likes you," I said.

"I wonder who he belongs to," Holly mused. "A kitten this small shouldn't be outside alone. Not in a storm like this."

There was another rumble of thunder overhead, and the kitten cringed and scooted next to Holly, rubbing up against her leg. Holly scooped up the drenched animal and stood. The cat didn't protest.

"Let's take him home and get him dried off," Holly said. She stepped past me and stood by the door. The rain was coming down harder now, running off the roof in sheets.

I turned and was about to pick up the umbrella from the ground when I noticed a small, glimmering object partially buried in the damp dirt. It was in a place that had been covered over by one of the wooden boxes.

And even before I reached down to pick it up, I knew what it was.

"Wow!" I exclaimed. I bent over and snatched up the object.

Holly turned. "What is—"

She stopped speaking when I held out my palm. *"Holy cow!"* she exclaimed.

In my hand was an old silver dollar.

At that very moment, I knew two things for sure. Number one: I knew that this dollar was part of the loot that the robbers had stolen.

And number two: I knew that the Adventure Club was going to find the rest of it.

3

Holly and I were still standing in the shed. Outside, the rain dumped so hard I thought it was going to crush the flimsy building that we were in. Thunder groaned, and the kitten in Holly's arms squirmed in fear.

"Shhhh," Holly said to the cat, holding it close. Then she spoke to me. "You found that coin right there on the ground?" she asked.

I nodded, still staring at the silver dollar. "Yeah," I said. "Right down there."

I knelt down again, inspecting the place where I had found the coin.

"Wow!" I shouted. I snapped my hand out, dug into

the ground a bit . . . and withdrew still *another* silver dollar!

I have to admit, I went a little bit crazy after that. I fell to my knees and pawed at the ground, searching for more. Holly knelt down and held the wet kitten in one arm, searching the ground with the other.

"There's got to be more!" I exclaimed. "There's got to be!"

Neither of us had any luck, but that didn't bother us. We knew we were on the trail of the stolen loot, and it would only be a matter of time before we found it.

"Let's call an emergency meeting of the Adventure Club," I said. "The six of us might have better luck searching together!"

"Yeah," Holly agreed. "But first we have to take this little guy back to my house and get him dried off."

At Holly's house, I called everyone on the phone while Holly dried off the kitten. She warmed up some milk in the microwave, and soon the little cat was snuggled up on a large, fluffy towel, sleeping.

Everyone I spoke with on the phone wanted to know what the big deal was. I wouldn't tell them.

"Just be at the clubhouse at five o'clock this afternoon," I said. "Rain or shine. This is important."

"It better be," said club president Shane Mitchell.

"Especially if it's still raining like it is now."

Five o'clock came. Thankfully, the rain had stopped. Holly and I were the first ones to arrive at our clubhouse, which is built up off the ground in a group of maple trees on the other side of McArdle's farm, just outside of town. A rope ladder dangled from above and I scurried up to the fort, climbing through a special hole in the floor. Holly had brought the kitten with her, and she was able to put the tiny creature in the pocket of her windbreaker and climb up the rope ladder.

Lyle Haywood was the next member to arrive.

"What's the big deal?" he asked. "Why are we meeting on a Saturday?"

"We'll tell you in a minute," I replied, "when everyone else gets here."

Club president Shane Mitchell showed up, and he asked the same question. I gave him the same answer I had given Lyle.

Tony Gritter arrived, and finally, Dylan Bunker. Dylan was fifteen minutes late as usual. Shane called the meeting to order as soon as Dylan's mop of red hair popped up through the floor.

"Okay Parker," he said to me. "What's up?"

I looked at Holly. She had a smug grin on her face.

I grinned, too.

"We all know about the old abandoned shed on Oak Street," I began. Everyone nodded, and I continued. "Well, Holly and I were there this morning. We found something."

When I said this, Holly reached into her pocket and pulled out the kitten. It had fallen asleep earlier, but now it was awake. Its eyes were half open and the creature was groggy.

"A *cat?*" Tony said in disgust. "You found a *cat* and you called a *meeting?"*

I was still smiling, and so was Holly. "Yeah, we found that kitten there," I said. "But that's not all. Dylan, hold out your hand."

Dylan was seated on an overturned milk crate next to me, and he showed me his pudgy palm. Without letting anyone else in the club see what I had in my hand, I placed one of the silver dollars in his palm, then I pulled his fingers over into a fist, concealing the coin from view. Dylan himself didn't even know what was in his hand.

"That's what we found," I said smartly.

Everyone was curious now, and they all leaned forward to see what Dylan had in his fist.

"Now open your hand, Dylan," I said.

As he did, you could hear a pin drop. When everyone saw the silver dollar in Dylan's palm, time seemed to stop. Nobody breathed. It was like all of the air had suddenly been sucked out of our clubhouse. Time stood still.

Finally, Shane stepped forward. His eyes were gigantic.

"It's . . . it's—"

"—It's part of the stolen loot!" I said, finishing his sentence for him. "But wait."

I dug into my pocket and pulled out the other silver dollar that we found, then I flipped it up into the air. Lyle Haywood reached out and grabbed it before it fell to the floor.

"Another one?!?!?" he exclaimed. "How many did you find?"

"That's it," I said, shaking my head. "We only found those two. Holly and I looked, but those were all we found. We figured that we would get everybody together, then we might have better luck finding the rest of the stolen money."

Shane was still holding the heavy coin in his hand. His eyes were glowing, and as he gazed at the dollar, he looked like he was hypnotized.

"All in favor of searching for the treasure, raise your hand," he said. His eyes never left the coin in his palm.

Tony walked over to the hole in the floor where the rope ladder was. He slipped through and began to climb down.

"You guys can hang out here and vote," he smirked, "but I'm going to go find *me* a pile of money."

"I second that!" Lyle replied, raising his hand. We scrambled, chattering like silly monkeys as we each took our turn climbing down the rope ladder.

The great treasure hunt was about to begin.

4

It didn't take us more than five minutes to race to the old shed.

Holly and I showed everyone where we had found the coins, and after a quick search without finding anything of interest, we decided we'd have to remove all of the junk and old debris so we could work better. It would be easier if we didn't have a bunch of old wooden boxes in our way.

In a few minutes, the shed was empty. There were piles and piles of junk heaped up outside, and the six of us got to work searching the old shed.

"We need a metal detector," Shane said.

"That would be great," agreed Holly, "but they cost a lot of money."

Tony kneeled to the ground and began digging in the dirt. "Hey," he said. "If there are any more silver dollars around here, I'm going to find them."

Lyle stared up at the rafters, like he was looking for some clue from above. Shane and Dylan began digging in the dirt next to Tony. Holly inspected the ground near the walls, looking for anything that would resemble a silver dollar. She was still carrying the kitten in the pocket of her coat, and once in a while the animal would pop out its head and look around. I dropped to my knees and joined Tony, Shane, and Dylan.

We dug as much as we could with our hands, but we couldn't dig very deep. Soon, my hands were as brown as the dirt I was scooping.

"Man, we're getting nowhere fast," Dylan said. He stopped digging and looked up, shrugging in disappointment. He sighed. "There's nothing here."

Lyle was still looking up into the rafters. Now his arms were crossed, and he was deep in thought.
"You're right, Dylan," he said, adjusting his glasses with a pointed finger.

Tony stopped digging and looked up at Lyle. "Well,

maybe if you'd quit staring off into space and help us out, we might find the loot a little bit quicker," he sneered.

"They weren't that dumb," Lyle said, ignoring Tony's jibe.

"*Who* wasn't that dumb?" Dylan asked.

"The robbers," Lyle replied. "I mean . . . sure, it was pretty dumb to rob a bank in the first place. But think about it. They came here to Great Bear Heart because it's a small town. They thought they would be able to hide for a while without getting caught. They had a plan, and they thought very carefully about where they would hide the money until things cooled down."

"Then why did Dylan find a silver dollar in the secret tunnel below the library?" Shane asked.

"And why did we find two silver dollars right here in the shed?" I asked. "I mean . . . if they were so smart, why were they so careless?"

Tony returned to digging, although without much enthusiasm. Lyle looked down and spoke.

"Because they didn't plan on getting caught," he answered. "They had planned for everything, just in case. But I don't think they really *believed* they would be found out in such a small town. They were forced to change their plans. I guarantee you that we won't find any more silver dollars in this shed. I think the two coins you found today, and the one Dylan found in the tunnel beneath the library had been dropped by accident. Now, the money might be around here somewhere in Great Bear Heart, but we're not going to find it in this old shed."

Shane and I had returned to digging, joining Tony. I didn't notice it at first, but Tony was digging faster.

"I would suspect that the robbers hid the money somewhere else," Lyle continued. "They just wouldn't leave—"

Lyle stopped speaking. Tony had suddenly stopped digging, and his hands began sweeping back and forth really fast.

He was brushing dirt off of something!

"What is it?" Dylan asked.

Tony didn't answer. We all drew closer to him, peering at what he had found.

Suddenly he plunged his hands into the soft earth. With a tug and a grunt, he pulled a large, rectangular object from the ground.

A briefcase.

5

A cold silence fell upon the shed. Tony Gritter held up the briefcase like it was a block of gold. We all just stared.

The briefcase was dirty and warped, and there was no doubt that it was very old and had been in the ground for a long time. We looked on in amazement.

Finally, Tony spoke.

"So . . . you were saying, Lyle?" he said, grinning at Lyle.

"Let's open it!" I exclaimed.

"Yeah!" said Holly. She had pulled the kitten from her pocket, and now the creature was cradled gently in her arms.

"I'll bet it's packed with silver dollars!" Dylan chimed.

Tony lowered the briefcase to the ground and began fumbling with the latches. We all huddled even closer.

"Hurry!" Dylan urged.

"Chill out, Dylan," Tony said. "These latches are old, and they're caked with dirt."

There was an audible *snap!* and one of the latches popped. Tony fumbled with the other one.

Snap!

Suddenly, it was so quiet in the shed that you could have heard a mouse burp. I don't think any of us moved a muscle or even breathed.

Tony grasped the lid of the briefcase, and lifted.

The briefcase was empty!

The six of us sighed in disappointment. I was really hoping that we had hit the jackpot.

"There's nothing in it!" Holly exclaimed.

"Why would someone bury an *empty* briefcase?" Shane wondered aloud.

"Let me see," Lyle said. Tony moved over, and Lyle knelt down in front of the briefcase. I knelt down right behind Lyle and looked over his shoulder.

The inside of the briefcase was beige, the color of beach sand. The leather was rippled and aged, but, all in all, it was in fairly good shape. There were several pockets and pouches for storing papers and documents. Lyle reached out and peered carefully into the compartments.

"There's more to this than what we're seeing," he said. "There has to be. Nobody would bury a briefcase without a reason . . . unless they were trying to hide something."

"Maybe someone already found the loot," I presumed. "Maybe they found the silver dollars, took them, and re-buried the case."

Lyle shook his head. "Maybe," he agreed, "but I don't think so." He was still fumbling through the pockets of the old case.

"Maybe it was just put there as a decoy," Shane speculated. "You know . . . to throw someone off."

"Nope," Lyle said, shaking his head. Suddenly, his hand emerged from one of the pouches.

He was holding an envelope.

Another stunned silence washed over the six of us. First, we had been excited when Tony found the briefcase, only to be disappointed to find that it didn't contain any silver coins.

Now, Lyle had found an envelope inside the briefcase, and our excitement was soaring again.

"Open it up!" Tony exclaimed.

The envelope was yellowed with age, and Lyle opened it carefully and removed a folded piece of paper. He placed the envelope inside the briefcase, unfolded the paper, and began to read.

6

"Bear, Face, Face, bee," Lyle read out loud.

"Huh?" Dylan Bunker quizzed.

"That's all it says," Lyle replied, flipping it over to see if there was anything written on the other side. There wasn't, and he held out the paper for all of us to see.

"Bear, Face, Face, bee," Holly read, leaning closer to the paper. She read it again. "Bear, Face, Face, bee. What's that supposed to mean?"

"It must be some kind of clue," I said. "Maybe it's some sort of coded message."

"I'll bet if we figure it out, we'll find the stolen loot!" Dylan exclaimed, his eyes shining. "We'll all be rich!"

We all racked our brains trying to figure out what it meant.

Bear, Face, Face, bee, I thought. What could *that* mean?

"Dylan is right," Lyle said. "If we can find out what this means, I'll bet we'll find where the silver dollars are hidden."

"But what if it's not?" Shane asked. "I mean, what if the briefcase and the note have nothing to do with the stolen money at all?"

"Well, let's look at the facts," Lyle replied. "We know that the robbers hopped a train from Detroit."

"Right," I agreed.

"We know that they hid out for a while in the tunnel beneath the library. And we all know that the money isn't in the tunnel."

That was true. After Dylan Bunker had discovered the silver dollar in the tunnel beneath the library, we searched and searched . . . but we didn't find any more.

Lyle continued. "We know that the robbers were discovered by the police, and they were chased up the hill. There was a shoot-out in this very shed. The bank robbers were killed, but the money was never found."

"How long did the bank robbers hide out in the tunnel?" Tony asked.

"A couple of weeks, I think," Lyle said.

"If that's true," Shane pondered, "then they would have had time to stash the cash anywhere in Great Bear Heart."

"That's right," Lyle nodded. "Maybe they hid it somewhere, thinking they could wait a while and then come back and get it."

"But they were discovered, and they never had a chance to come back and get the money," I said.

"I'll bet you're right, Parker," Lyle said to me. "I'll bet that the coins are hidden somewhere around town, maybe right beneath our noses. The robbers made this note to remind them where they hid the money, so they could come back and get it when the heat was off."

"But what does it mean?" Holly asked. She was gently stroking the cat's head.

"That's what we need to find out," Lyle replied. He looked at his watch. "It's already seven o'clock. We don't have much time tonight, but tomorrow we can begin."

"Hunting for the loot?" Dylan asked hopefully.

"In a roundabout way," Lyle replied. "We need to find out if anyone knows what this letter means."

"The Great Bear Heart Historical Museum!" I

exclaimed, snapping my fingers. "I'll bet there's a lot of information there!"

"Yeah!" said Holly. "They probably have all the old newspaper clippings about the robbery!"

We left the abandoned shed and returned to the clubhouse. Lyle carried the envelope and the letter, but we left the briefcase. We figured it wouldn't do us much good, anyway.

It was decided that we would meet at the clubhouse the next morning at eight a.m., sharp. From there, we would divide up into teams of two, and each pair would go and visit different places and people around town. There are a lot of people who have lived in Great Bear Heart for a long time, and we figured that maybe they might know what the cryptic note meant.

I went to bed that night, dreaming of shiny silver dollars. I just *knew* that we would find the stolen loot.

But what I didn't know was the fact that while we had been in the shed, someone had followed us.

7

Sunday started out just fine. I woke up at seven, nuked some oatmeal for breakfast, and got ready to meet everyone at the clubhouse. The day was sunny, and I just *knew* we were going to find the stolen silver dollars. There was no question in my mind.

At five minutes to eight, I hopped on my bicycle and began pedaling to McArdle's farm where our clubhouse was located. And of course, I would have to ride right past the old abandoned shed on Oak Street.

And that's where I spotted the Martin brothers. All three of them. Larry, Gary, and Terry.

Trouble . . . times *three.* The Martin brothers are

nothing but trouble makers, and if they were involved in anything, you can be sure they were up to no good.

But it was what they were doing that really bothered me.

All three of them had shovels . . . and they were digging up the yard all around the abandoned shed!

I was so stunned I stopped pedaling and let my bike coast to a stop. Gary saw me, and he stopped digging.

"What are you doing?!?!?!" I demanded. At the sound of my voice, Terry and Larry stopped digging, too. They looked at me with leering grins.

"What does it look like we're doing?" Gary sneered. "We're digging for worms," he continued, answering his own question.

"Yeah," Larry piped up. "And after we find some worms, we're going to dig all the way to China."

I should have expected as much from the Martin brothers. They are nothing but trouble-making smart-alecks.

"We heard you guys talking about the stolen money," Terry said.

"What?!?!?" I exclaimed. "I don't know what you're talking about!"

"Gary, here, heard every word you guys said last

night, didn't you, Gary?"

Gary laughed and nodded, and grinned like a snake. "Every word. I saw you guys doing stuff in here in the shed, so I snuck up from behind and listened against the wall. I heard all about the two old silver dollars that you and Holly found. And guess what we found?"

At this, Terry walked into the shed and emerged a moment later carrying the briefcase that we had discovered.

"We know that you found something in that case," Gary continued. "I didn't hear exactly what, but I know that you guys are going to hunt for that loot today. But we're going to find it *first.*"

I was furious. Gary Martin had been spying on us! He had been listening the whole time last night!

I sped away on my bike, heading out to the clubhouse. My mind was spinning like a top.

And I was *mad.* This wasn't the first time the Martin brothers had caused a problem for us, and it probably wouldn't be the last.

My bike bounced across the field. As I approached the clump of maples that supported our clubhouse high in the air, I counted four other bikes. Everyone was there except me, and, I presumed, Dylan.

I hopped off my bike and flew to the rope ladder. In seconds, my head had popped up through the square opening in the floor of the tree fort.

"A new bike, that's what I'm going to get," Tony was saying. "You know . . . one that I can race and go over jumps. That's what I'm going to buy!"

Holly O'Mara, cradling the kitten in her arms like she had the day before, turned and looked at me. My face must have showed my anger, because she frowned and said "Hey Parker . . . what's up with *you?*"

I climbed up into the fort and took my seat on an overturned milk crate.

"The Martin brothers!" I said, gasping for breath. "They know what we're doing! They know about the treasure!"

Shane Mitchell came up off his milk crate.

"What?!?!" he exclaimed. *"How?!?!"*

"Gary was spying on us!" I replied. "Last night! While we were in the shed!"

"Say *what?!?!"* Lyle exclaimed. "How? When?"

I took a breath, then let it out. "It's true!" I panted. "They're over at the shed right now. They're digging up the entire yard with shovels!"

"They aren't going to find anything there!" Holly

said.

"Maybe not," I huffed, "but the problem is that they *know.* They *know* that the stolen money is hidden somewhere in Great Bear Heart."

"Big deal," Tony remarked. "*Lots* of people know. Even my *dad* knows about it. It's part of the town's history."

"Yeah," I said with a frown, "but up until last night, that's all it was. A story. Old history. Now the Martins know the same thing that we do . . . those silver dollars are *real.* And they're stashed somewhere around Great Bear Heart."

There was a sudden noise from below, and the sound of heavy breathing. A pudgy hand appeared in the hole in the floor, and then another. Dylan's mop of red hair popped up.

"Hey guys," he said, out of breath from the climb. "Sorry I'm late. What'd I miss?"

No one said a single thing. We were all staring at Shane. He was looking up, stroking his chin.

And he was *smiling.*

Dylan climbed up into the clubhouse and took a seat, and we all waited and watched until Shane spoke.

"So," he began, "the Martins know that there are

silver dollars hidden somewhere in Great Bear Heart."

He paused for a long time, but he still had a grin on his face. Finally, he spoke again.

"Well, you know what?" he asked, still staring up at the ceiling. Since none of us knew what he was getting at, we remained silent.

"I think that the Martin brothers are about to make a discovery."

None of us knew what *that* meant, but I'll tell you one thing for sure:

Shane Mitchell has a knack for coming up with good ideas. It's not the *only* reason he's president of the Adventure Club, but it's on the top ten.

And when I heard Shane's idea, I just about jumped off of my milk crate. So did Holly. And Dylan, and Tony, and Lyle.

The Martin brothers were about to get what they deserved.

8

"We need to find a way to lead the Martin brothers astray," Shane began. "You know . . . make them think that they're going to find the stolen money."

"But they'll just be wasting their time," Dylan protested.

"That's what he's talking about," Tony shot back. "We need to make the Martins waste time going off in a direction that won't lead anywhere."

"Exactly," Shane replied with a snap of his fingers. "That will give us more time to find the real loot ourselves."

"We could make up a fake map," I offered.

"Yeah!" Holly agreed. She set the kitten down on the floor of our fort and continued. "We can create a map for them to find! They'll think it's the 'real' map, and start looking for the stolen money!"

"And we can even make a 'treasure' for them to find!" Lyle said. "They'll think that they actually found the treasure until they open it up!"

"Until they open what up?" Dylan asked.

Lyle shrugged. "I don't know. Whatever we decide to use as a treasure chest."

Shane snapped his fingers again. "I've got it!" he said. "My dad has a really old toolbox. I mean, it's *old.* It's all rusty and beat-up. We can stash it somewhere, and then create a map leading to it. Then, we can 'accidentally' drop the map when we know the Martin brothers are watching. They'll pick it up and—"

"The Martins will think it's the real map!" I exclaimed.

"They'll think we dropped it by *accident!*" shrieked Dylan.

"And they'll set out to find the treasure!" Holly cried.

Shane nodded, and his eyes were aflame. "You got it!" he said. "They won't know that the map is bogus!"

"But where are we going to hide the toolbox?" Tony

asked. "I mean . . . it has to be someplace good."

"Yeah," I agreed. "And we have to put something special inside the toolbox. Something like a note that says *'hahaha! The joke's on YOU!'* or something."

We thought about that for a minute. Whatever we were going to put in the toolbox, it had to be *good.* We really wanted to get the Martin brothers once and for all.

All of a sudden, Shane slapped his hand to his forehead. He started laughing so hard that he fell off his milk crate and doubled over on the clubhouse floor.

"What?!?!?" Tony asked. "What's so funny?!?! What are you going to put in the toolbox?!?!"

Shane was laughing so hard he couldn't speak. When he finally got hold of himself, he sat up and leaned against the wall. Tears were running down his cheeks.

"My neighbor had a small animal living under his house," he said, in between chokes of laughter. "He put out a live trap and caught it last night, and he's going to take the animal way out into the woods and let it go."

Dylan raised his eyebrows and shrugged. "So?"

"Well, we're going to put that creature in the toolbox," Shane said, and he began laughing like crazy again, slapping his legs with his hands.

We couldn't figure out what was so funny.

"What kind of animal is it?" Dylan asked.

"Yeah," I quizzed. "Is the animal supposed to scare them?"

Suddenly, Lyle grinned. Holly's eyes lit up, and the two of them started to laugh.

"Shane! That's perfect!" Holly exclaimed.

"Come on, guys!" Dylan whined. "What's so funny?"

"It's a SKUNK!" Holly and Lyle both cried in unison. Shane could only acknowledge with a nod before breaking into another fit of bellowing laughter. We all starting roaring, and soon all of us were rolling on the floor of the clubhouse, laughing so hard we couldn't see straight.

The Martin brothers were going to find a treasure, all right. A smelly treasure . . . courtesy of the Adventure Club.

9

Each of us had special instructions. Tony Gritter and Dylan Bunker were in charge of getting Shane's dad's toolbox ready. Holly and I were in charge of creating a map that would lead the Martin brothers to a 'secret' spot, where they would find the 'treasure'. It wasn't easy, either. We had to make the map look authentic, like it had been written a long time ago. I used a piece of white paper, but it looked too new. There's no way the Martin's would believe that it was written years and years ago.

I drew the map as simple as I could, knowing that the Martins weren't that smart. The easier it would be for them to find the treasure, the better. But I spent a lot of time on it, drawing pictures of landmarks like trees and the lake and some of the buildings in town. For the location of the 'treasure chest', I picked an old outhouse near Massasauga Swamp, not far from where Lyle and Holly had crashed an experimental plane that we'd made. I figured we could stash the toolbox, skunk and all, inside the old outhouse. No one goes there anymore, and it would be a perfect place to stash the fake treasure.

"Hey," Holly said, holding the note up in her hands. We were in my dad's garage, seated at his workbench. There were lots of tools scattered about on the wood surface, a can of motor oil, and several cans of paint that had dribble marks down their sides. She'd brought the kitten over and placed it on the bench. The cat wandered aimlessly, curiously inspecting tools and other odds and ends.

"What?" I asked.

"Rub the paper on the cement floor," she said. "That might scuff it up a bit."

I hopped down from the stool and took the map from Holly, then I placed it on the cement floor and stepped on it, pushing it around in a circular fashion. Then I picked it up. There were scratch marks on the paper, but it still looked too new.

"Now try crumpling it up and then un-crumpling it," Holly suggested.

I wadded up the map tightly in my hand and packed it into my palm. The paper made a crinkling sound as I pulled the edges out until the map was un-crumpled.

"Not bad," I said, inspecting the wrinkled map, "but it's still too white. It needs to look older."

"Let me see it," Holly said, holding out her hand. I held the map out, but she dropped it. It slipped through her fingers and began to float to the cement floor. I moved quick to grab it. The sudden motion scared the kitten, and it leapt into Holly's arms . . . but not before it bumped into the can of motor oil. I tried to grab it before it tipped over, but I was too late. The gooey, honey-colored liquid spilled all over the workbench and began dribbling over the side of the table . . . and right onto the map I had drawn!

"Oh no!" I gasped, leaping from the stool to the cement floor. I snatched up the map. *"Oh no!"* I repeated. The map was soaked with motor oil, and the greasy fluid dripped from the paper as I held it up.

"I'm sorry," Holly said sheepishly. "I should have been watching the kitten."

"It wasn't your fault," I said. "And the kitten didn't mean to do it. But if—"

I stopped speaking, and stared at the stained note on the cement floor. "Hold everything!" I said. "I'll bet it'll work!"

"What?" she asked. "What will work?!?!"

I didn't answer her. Instead, I grabbed a rag from dad's bench. Then I placed the map down and wiped away the oil.

"Go into my house and get my mom's hair dryer from the bathroom. The hand-held one that looks like a gun. Go get it, quick!"

Holly returned a moment later with the dryer. I plugged it into an outlet behind the workbench, holding the map in one hand and the blow dryer in the other. Warm air made the paper waver. In a few minutes, the paper was dry . . . or as dry as it was going to get, anyway.

But what was even better: the map looked beat-up. It looked old and tarnished . . . like a *real* treasure map!

"Parker!" Holly exclaimed. "That looks *perfect!"*

And it did. The oil stain gave the paper an old, greasy look, like the paper had been out in the weather for a long, long, time. My carefully drawn map had smudges and smears . . . just like you'd expect from an old treasure map.

"Good going, kitty!" I said.

Holly placed the kitten on the workbench. "Actually, I think we just got lucky."

"Lucky or not, this is going to work! Come on! Let's head over to Tony Gritter's house!"

While we were working on the map, Tony and Dylan had been working on the toolbox.

"That'll work," Tony was telling Dylan as we rode up

to the Gritter's on our bicycles. He was holding up the toolbox, admiring his handiwork. Using a hand-drill, he'd punctured the metal box with a dozen holes on the end. Each hole was about the size of the head of a pin, and the skunk would have plenty of air to breathe.

"Where's Lyle?" Dylan asked. Lyle's job was to go down to the library to try and find out more about the strange, cryptic message that we'd found on the note in the shed.

"He's still down at the library I think," Holly said with a nod over her shoulder.

"That's fine," Tony said. "Let's get this box over to Shane's."

We would have to act fast. Shane's neighbor planned on releasing the skunk when he returned from work that evening. We had to get the skunk into the toolbox (which I had *no* idea how we were going to do without getting sprayed ourselves), then we would have to carry it to the outhouse near Massasauga Swamp. Of course, we had to somehow get the 'bogus' treasure map to the Martin brothers. Hopefully, they would go looking for the treasure right away. I guessed that if they followed my map like I'd planned, it would probably take them about ten minutes to reach the swamp.

When we arrived at Shane's house, he was sitting on the front porch, sipping a glass of lemonade. Next to him was an aluminum crate that was twice the size of a shoe box. There were small holes on the sides and on each end, and, although I couldn't really see inside, I could see some sort of movement within. We were a few feet away, and I could smell the faint scent of skunk in the air.

"Don't tell me the skunk's in there," Tony said, pointing an accusing finger at the metal trap that sat on the wood porch.

Shane nodded. "It sure is," he replied knowingly.

"But how come he doesn't spray his smelly smell all over the place?" Dylan asked curiously.

"It's a special kind of trap just for skunks," Shane explained. "See . . . the only way a skunk can spray you is when he raises his tail. If he can't raise his tail, he can't spray you. This box is specially designed to keep a skunk from being able to raise its tail."

"Yeah, but how are we going to get him into the toolbox?" Holly asked.

Shane pointed to one end of the box. "All we have to do is open this end and stick it next to the toolbox. When the skunk comes out of the trap, he'll have nowhere to go *but* the toolbox. I'll close the lid real quick, and the top of the toolbox will keep his tail down." He closed the lid of the toolbox to demonstrate. "See?"

"That'll work!" Tony said.

"Of course it will," Shane said confidently. He stood up and held out his hands. "Give me the toolbox."

Tony had strapped the toolbox to the back of his bicycle and he retrieved it, handing it to Shane.

"Watch this," Shane replied, opening up the toolbox. The metal lid rotated on its hinges and banged on the wood porch. Then he gently picked up the live trap containing the skunk. We all took several steps back . . . just in case.

"Oh, you big sissies," he said, opening up the end of the trap and placing it almost inside the toolbox.

Suddenly, I saw a flash of black and white as the small creature poked his head out.

"That's it," Shane said. "Just a little bit more . . . ."

As if he understood what Shane was saying, the skunk took an apprehensive step outside of the trap—I could see its head poking out—and right into the toolbox. Shane quickly closed the lid of the toolbox . . . with the skunk safely inside.

Holly, Tony, Dylan and I let out a cheer, and Shane

bowed proudly. "All in a day's work," he said with a grin. Then he turned to me. "Parker, did you and Holly come up with a map?"

"Did we *ever!*" Holly replied, answering for me.

I pulled the tarnished paper from my pocket. Shane, Tony, and Dylan crowded around.

"That looks cool!" Tony said. "It looks really old! How did you do it?"

"Actually, Dollar did it," Holly replied.

"Who?" Dylan asked.

"Yeah," I said, looking at Holly. "Who is 'Dollar'?"

Holly gently pulled the kitten from the pocket of her sweatshirt. "Him. I'm going to call him 'Dollar', since he was the reason we found those two silver dollars in the first place."

"Cool," Shane said. "I've always wanted a club mascot."

The kitten yawned, and Holly returned it to her pocket.

"Where does the map lead to?" Dylan asked.

I pointed to a spot on the map. "I thought the best place to hide the toolbox with the skunk would be the old outhouse near Massasauga Swamp," I replied.

"Great idea!" Shane said. "We can put it inside and

cover it with stuff. We don't want to make it too hard for them to find. The Martin brothers aren't very bright."

Just then, Lyle came pedaling down the drive. His bike whizzed up to us and he leapt off. *Something* was up, that was for sure.

"What?!?!" I asked him. "Did you find out where the treasure is?!?!"

"No," Lyle gasped, out of breath. "But the Martin brothers are in the park right now! All three of them! It's the perfect time to walk by and drop the fake map! They'll be sure to see it and pick it up!"

"We've got to act fast," Shane ordered. "I'll take the toolbox to the outhouse. You guys take that map and make sure that the Martin brothers find it. I'll meet up with you on the trail to the swamp!"

Things were getting cranked up. The Martins were going to find a treasure, all right . . . a treasure that would leave them stinking to high heaven.

10

Shane scooped up the toolbox containing the skunk and headed for the swamp. The rest of us sprang into action with a simple plan.

All we were going to do was walk by the park quickly, chattering and talking excitedly to one another. When we walked past the Martin brothers, I was going to 'accidentally' drop the map. The five of us would keep talking, pretending not to notice the paper that had fallen to the ground. Hopefully, the Martins would spot it and investigate after we'd passed by.

Down at the park, Gary, Terry, and Larry were busy doing what they do best: goofing off. They were down near the water trying to push each other in.

We walked along the old railroad bed that passed right by the Great Bear Heart Public Library, which used to be the old train depot.

"Okay," I said. *"Everyone start talking. Let's make it look like we're real excited."*

We began talking among ourselves, bragging about how we knew where the loot was and what we were going to do with all of the money when we found it.

Gary Martin turned and saw us. He yelled something, but he was too far away and I couldn't understand what he said. We all ignored him anyway, just like we usually do. His shout drew the attention of his two brothers, and when they turned and looked, I dropped the map that Holly and I had created. I heard the paper crinkle and fall away.

And we never looked back. We kept on walking and talking until the Martins were out of sight, then we ducked into the woods and made a circle up the hill, making sure that the brothers weren't watching us.

Suddenly, Dylan stopped and pointed.

"Look!" he exclaimed, pointing into the distance.

On the other side of the library, the three Martins were standing on the old railroad bed. They were huddled together—and Terry was holding the map in his hands!

We couldn't hear what they were saying to one another, but by their expressions and their movements, we could tell that they were pretty excited.

"It's going to work!" I exclaimed. "They fell for it hook, line, and sinker!"

"You mean hook, line and *stinker!*" Tony said, and we started laughing so hard we almost fell to the ground.

Then the Martins looked around to see if they were being watched, or wondering if we had noticed the map was missing and were coming back for it.

Then they started running. They sprinted across the small parking lot and slowed when they reached the road, checking briefly to make sure no one was coming. Then they darted across the road and headed up the hill.

"Where are they going?" I wondered aloud. "The swamp is the other way."

"I'll bet they're going home first," Lyle replied. "I'll bet they're going to go home and then head out to the swamp."

"Lyle is right," Holly mused. "They probably think the treasure is buried, so they're going to get a shovel. I'll bet they're going home first, and then head straight for

Massasauga Swamp."

I think that this was about the time that we all forgot about looking for the treasure, and became focused on watching the Martin brothers open up that toolbox with the skunk inside. Boy, were they in for a surprise!

"Come on!" Tony said. "Let's find Shane and get to the swamp before they do and hide in the woods. This is going to be great!"

We hustled through a few back yards to a narrow trail that wound through the woods. Massasauga Swamp isn't that far away, but we'd have to hurry if we wanted to find a place to hide before the Martins showed up.

We were almost to the swamp when we met up with Shane. He was running toward us. When he saw us, he stopped and threw up his hands in exasperation.

"Man, what took you guys so long?" he asked. "The treasure . . . I mean the skunk . . . is in the outhouse!"

"And the Martins are on their way!" I said with a laugh. "This is going to be great!"

Lyle spotted a hiding place not far away from the old outhouse. It was a clump of small trees at the edge of the swamp. All of the branches were intertwined, tangled together in what appeared to be one big mass of weaving tentacles. The six of us could hide within and peer through the limbs without being spotted by the Martins.

And we found the hiding place just in time, too . . . because as soon as we had ducked down within the brush, we heard noises coming from the trail.

The Martin brothers were coming!

11

"There's Terry!" Holly whispered.

Sure enough, Terry Martin was leading the trio. As they approached, we could see that they were carrying shovels, just like Shane had speculated. Larry Martin was also carrying a large burlap bag. I guess they figured that they might need something to take home their treasure in.

"Boy, are they in for a surprise!" Dylan whispered.

"Quiet!" Tony hissed. *"If they hear us, the jig is up!"*

We watched in silence, our excitement and anticipation boiling beneath our skin. We couldn't wait for the Martins to find the 'treasure chest' and open it up!

Through the thick branches, we saw them stop on the trail. Gary Martin carried the map in his hand, and he unfolded it for a quick inspection.

"It's got to be right around here," he said, looking around. Larry and Terry now looked around as well, their heads swiveling about, peering around tree trunks and branches.

"There is supposed to be an old outhouse around here somewhere," Gary said, glancing down and reading the map.

"There is," Terry agreed. "I've seen it before. It was a long time ago, but I know that it's around here somewhere."

"Come on," Gary said, stuffing the map into the front pocket of his jeans. "Let's split up and look around."

And with that, the three Martins left the trail and began searching for the outhouse. Branches popped and cracked under their feet as they strode through the underbrush.

"The outhouse is right in front of their noses!" I whispered.

"Yeah," Shane agreed. *"But it's hidden behind those cedars. They'll find it soon enough!"*

Right now, however, the three Martin brothers were

walking in the opposite direction. I wanted to yell something like *'hey you goofs! It's right over there!'* but of course I didn't.

So we waited. We waited and we watched as the three Martins meandered through the brush.

"Anything yet?" Larry called out. He had walked so far into the brush that I couldn't see him.

"Nope!" Gary answered back loudly.

"Me neither!" Terry barked.

"Keep looking!" Gary ordered. "It's right around here somewhere!"

And he was right. The problem was, Gary was headed right for our hiding place. He was going to find something, all right . . . *but that something was going to be us!*

12

Branches cracked and snapped beneath Gary Martin's feet as he drew closer and closer to the thicket where the six of us were hiding. None of us moved, and I held my breath. If Gary kept walking in the same direction that he was headed, he was going to run right into us. Our hiding place was good, but if someone was real close they would spot us in a heartbeat.

My spirit sank. I was really looking forward to seeing the Martin brothers open up that old toolbox and find our little surprise inside. Now, however, it looked like our plan wasn't going to work, after all.

Five more steps. In five more steps, Gary Martin

would be so close that I would be able to bite his kneecap.

"I found it!" Larry Martin shouted. His excited cry echoed through the forest and caused Gary to spin. My heart flew.

He started walking the other way!

Whew. That had been a *close* one.

"I found it!" Larry called out again. *"It's here! It's really here!"*

From where we were, we could see the three Martin brothers gathered around the old outhouse.

"This is going to be good!" Lyle said quietly, rubbing his hands together in excitement.

Through the latticework of limbs and branches, we watched as Terry Martin swung open the door of the outhouse. Then he drew back.

"Eeeewww!" he exclaimed, holding his nose. "What's that smell?!?!"

"What do you expect, you ninny!" Gary Martin shot back. "It's an outhouse! It's got to be a hundred years old! Did you expect it to smell like roses?"

"That's really bad," Terry said, waving his hand beneath his nose in disgust.

"Well, hold your breath, then," Gary said, taking a

step away from the small structure. We could see him draw in a deep breath of fresh air. His chest swelled and his cheeks puffed out as he held it, turned, and entered the outhouse. Terry and Larry each backed away and took breaths, held their noses, and walked up to the door of the outhouse.

The tiny building wasn't big enough for all three of them to fit, but we knew it wouldn't matter anyway. Shane had placed the toolbox under a pile of old newspapers and Sears catalogs that must have been there for a hundred years; Gary wouldn't have any trouble finding the 'treasure'.

We could hear shuffling noises and scraping sounds coming from the outhouse.

"Find it yet?" Terry asked.

"Gimme a second," Gary's hollow voice echoed from inside the outhouse. Then, all of a sudden, he burst out the door carrying the old toolbox.

"It's here!" he exclaimed in a rush of escaping breath. Terry and Larry leapt back, each of them exhaling forcefully and joining Gary at his side.

"And those goofy kids didn't even know they lost the map!" Gary Martin gloated. "Hah! They did all of the work for us!"

"The joke is sure going to be on them!" Larry exclaimed. "Wait until they find out that *we* found the stolen loot!"

"Open it up! Open it up!" Terry begged. "I can't wait to see all of that money!"

"It's not very heavy," Gary said, leaning over and

placing the toolbox on the ground. From where we were hidden, we could no longer see the metal box at their feet.

"Well, it's probably all hundred dollar bills," Larry speculated. "That wouldn't be very heavy at all."

"Oh, man," I whispered. *"Are they ever in for a surprise!"*

"A smelly surprise!" Holly said quietly.

"You guys hush up!" Shane ordered. *"Gary's about to open the toolbox!"*

Gary had knelt down and was reaching for the box. Then Terry and Larry dropped to their knees as well.

"Guys, we are about to be filthy, stinking rich," Gary bragged, which nearly made all six of us bust out laughing. They were going to be stinking, all right . . . and as we looked on, Gary flipped the latch and opened the toolbox.

13

To say that Gary, Larry, and Terry Martin ran from the toolbox would not be correct.

They *exploded* away from the toolbox.

One second they were gathered around the old metal box, and in the next they were flying in all directions, screaming and hollering.

"SKUNK!" Larry Martin shrieked at the top of his lungs, but, of course, it was already too late. The creature had sprayed all three brothers, and at close range, too. We could hear them crashing and thrashing wildly through the woods, zig-zagging along the trail, putting as much distance as they could between them and the

offending, odorous creature.

Finally, when we knew that they couldn't hear us, the six of us in the Adventure Club blew up in a fit of laughter. Shane fell to the ground, bellowing and chortling. Holly O'Mara was laughing so hard she had tears in her eyes. Dylan had leapt to his feet, and he was jumping up and down in the air. *"Yes! Yes! YES!"* he was shouting, over and over again.

Tony, Lyle and I slapped our palms together, sharing high-fives.

"That . . . that . . . that was . . . was . . . AWESOME!" Shane spluttered.

"Did you see the look on Gary's face when he ran?!?!" Tony exclaimed. "He looked like he'd seen a ghost!"

"Yeah!" Lyle said, removing his glasses from his face. "A black and white ghost!"

"A smelly, stinky, black and white ghost!" I replied, holding my nose.

"I think that was better than the prank at Devil's Ridge," Dylan said. His hands were still in the air, but he had stopped bouncing up and down. We had played a joke on the Martins at an old cemetery that we'd discovered, and we scared the tar out of all three of them.

"Nah, that was better," Tony replied. "But Operation Stinky Boys was pretty good."

Tony's comment brought another round of choking laughter. From that day on, whenever we talked about the prank, we called it *'Operation Stinky Boys.'* Even to this day I smile when I think of Terry, Larry and Gary fleeing frantically through the woods.

But the episode was far from over.

We were all laughing and whooping it up, congratulating each other for being so smart, for giving the Martin brothers something they really deserved, that we failed to notice something.

Holly was the first to spot it, the first to stop laughing. I saw her peering through the branches. She wasn't smiling. In fact, her face had gone from an expression of happiness to that of horror.

And when I saw what she was looking at, I, too, was gripped by the paralyzing hand of fear.

While we had been laughing and joking and having a good time, we forgot about one very important thing:

The skunk.

He had wandered right toward us, wobbling through the weeds and the brush—and now he was only a few feet away!

14

I saw the look on Holly's face and I followed her gaze to see what she was staring at. When I saw the skunk, my laughter ended abruptly, and I gasped. Everyone else suddenly stopped laughing, and when they saw the skunk bobbling through the brush there was a moment of horrified silence. No one moved, no one spoke. The only thing we could hear were a few birds in the trees . . . and the subtle cracks and pops of leaves and twigs as the cat-sized rodent slowly ambled toward us.

And then, in sudden realization, we knew that if we didn't act fast, all six of us were going to wind up just as stinky and smelly as the Martin brothers.

"Run!" Tony shouted, and his voice echoed through the forest. In history class, we read about Paul Revere, and how he rode a horse through Lexington at night, shouting *'The British are coming! The British are coming!'* Tony's shriek reminded me of that.

In a split-second, the six of us were on our feet, falling over one another, bumping into each other, smacking into branches, trying to flee as fast as we could. Holly bumped into me and I almost fell. I caught myself just in time and dove through a net of leafy branches, heading in the opposite direction of the skunk. Dylan fell face-first into a bush, but he rolled to the side, bounded up, and ran as fast as he could.

In a few seconds we were far enough away from the skunk, and we slowed to a walk. I was out of breath, and so was everyone else. My chest was heaving as I gasped for air, and I followed behind Lyle as the six of us made our way through the dense shrubs and branches.

After a few moments, we reached the trail. I kept glancing nervously over my shoulder, making sure that the skunk wasn't following us. It wasn't, of course, and I don't know what we would have done if it was.

Then we all started laughing again. Sure, we'd had a close call, but we had escaped without suffering the smelly consequences.

"That'll teach 'em!" Tony exclaimed.

"You bet!" Dylan replied.

"I'll bet they stink up the whole town!" I said.

"Or worse!" said Holly.

We laughed and giggled and joked all the way home.

Nobody saw or heard anything from the Martin brothers for a week. We all thought that their parents had probably shipped them off to Timbuktu until they got rid of the skunk smell.

But there was still one problem: we weren't any closer to finding the stolen money. The only clue we had was a cryptic note that we'd found in the briefcase. Even the lady who ran the Great Bear Heart Historical Museum didn't know what the words written on the note had meant.

At the next regular meeting of the Adventure Club, we voted to suspend our search.

"We could waste the whole summer looking for that treasure," Tony said. "And we might not even find it."

"And besides," I said, "maybe someone has already found it. We'd be spending all of our time for nothing."

Holly laughed. "I don't care if we ever find the money," she said. "Just seeing the Martins get sprayed by that skunk was worth more than gold!"

We all laughed. *Operation Stinky Boys* was something that none of us would ever, ever forget.

"So now what are we going to do?" Dylan asked. "I mean . . . the purpose of the Adventure Club is to have cool adventures. What are we going to do next?"

None of us really had any idea. We all just sat there, staring off into space, trying to think of something fun to do. Dollar the cat was batting around an acorn with his paws. Other than that, nobody moved.

Well, we'd be finding something to do, all right—because the Martin brothers were mad. They knew that we were the ones that had put that skunk in the toolbox.

And they were about to take revenge.

15

One of the things that we were most proud of was our tree fort. We built it last summer, high in a tree in McArdle's field, using scrap lumber. It wasn't very big, and wasn't much to look at—just a single-room fort with a hole in the floor to climb through—but it was *ours*. The six of us worked really hard, and we were all proud of it when we had finished.

We all had agreed to meet at the clubhouse on Saturday morning for our weekly meeting. I walked over to Holly's house. She was waiting for me on the porch. Dollar sat next to her. The cat had become very faithful and loyal, following Holly wherever she went.

"Well, what do you think we're going to do?" Holly asked as she stood up.

"I'm not sure," I replied. "But Lyle was saying something about finding our submarine in the lake and fixing it."

"That would be awesome!" Holly exclaimed.

Earlier in the summer, we found an old submarine in the junkyard. We fixed it up and took it exploring in Puckett Lake. We even found an underwater tunnel that led all the way to Lake Huron!

But the sub had sprung a leak in Puckett Lake, and the six of us had barely escaped with our lives. We thought it would be cool to find the old sub, fix it up, and take it out on more adventures.

We talked as we walked to the outskirts of town, until we reached McArdle's field.

Right away, we knew something wasn't quite right.

In the field, at the bottom of the tree beneath our clubhouse, stood Shane Mitchell, Tony Gritter, and Lyle Haywood.

"Why aren't they in the fort?" Holly asked.

I shrugged. "I don't know," I replied.

When we drew closer, it became even more obvious that something was very, very wrong. Shane looked angry. Tony was clenching and unclenching his fists. Even Lyle, who is pretty calm, looked like he was about to explode.

"Hey guys," I said as we approached. "What's the matter?"

Shane, Lyle, and Tony said nothing. Instead, they all just turned their heads and looked up. Tony pointed, and Holly and I looked up.

I gasped, and Holly's hands flew to her mouth. I thought she was going to cry.

"Oh no!" I said.

The clubhouse . . . the fort that we'd all worked so very hard to build . . . was destroyed.

16

We were devastated.

High above us, the clubhouse was in shambles. Boards had been torn away, and some of them were broken. Some of the boards had fallen to the ground, and they were scattered around the trunk of the tree. The rope ladder had been cut, and it lay coiled like a snake in the grass. Even the milk crates that we used as chairs had been destroyed. It looked like someone had beat them with a hammer.

Dylan Bunker showed up fifteen minutes late, and he just stared. I think a tear came to his eye. He really looked like he was about to cry.

It was obvious that someone had deliberately wrecked our clubhouse—and I'll give you one guess who was responsible.

"The Martin brothers did this!" Shane huffed. "I know they did!"

Tony clenched a fist with his right hand and punched the palm of his other. "When I get my hands on those guys, I'm gonna—"

"Hold on, hold on," Lyle said. "We can't just accuse somebody just because we *think* we know who did it."

"But who else would do such a thing?" Holly said.

"Lyle is right," I said. "We need to be able to prove that the Martins were involved. Right now, we don't have any proof. If we can prove they did this, then—"

"Then we could go to the police," Shane said.

Now *that* was a good idea.

Problem was, we searched and searched, but we still didn't have any proof that the Martins were involved. Oh, we all knew that they were the ones who had destroyed our clubhouse . . . but we just couldn't *prove* it.

Lyle is really good at climbing trees, and he scurried up the trunk of the tree to get a first-hand look at the damage. His report wasn't very good.

"It's totaled," he said when he'd climbed back down.

"And I didn't find any clue that would link the damage to the Martins."

That was bad news. Not only was it bad news, but the reality of our situation began to sink in. We'd have to build another clubhouse . . . which, of course, would be a huge project, and cost more money than we had.

Finally, after a long while, we began walking back to town. No one said a word. We were all really, really angry . . . and very sad.

But before we reached town, who do you think we saw coming toward us on bicycles?

The Martins.

Gary, Terry, and Larry.

As they drew closer, I could feel my anger rising. Tony was fuming, and I could hear him breathing hard. Tony is a pretty good sized guy, and I certainly wouldn't want to get into a fight with him.

But the Martins were older. They were older . . . and bigger.

The three brothers rode up to us and stopped. Gary was holding an ice cream cone. Terry and Larry were munching on candy bars.

"So," Gary sneered as he licked his ice cream. "No meeting today?"

"You guys are gonna get it if it's the last thing we do," Holly fumed.

"Shut up, you dumb girl," Larry snapped.

That was all it took. Tony stepped forward, doubled up his fists, and raised them to his chest.

"That's it!" he said. "Nobody calls any of my friends 'dumb'!" And with that, he swung his arm . . . and smashed Gary Martin's ice cream cone right into his face!

Shane and Lyle leapt forward and grabbed Tony before things got worse. They pulled him back. Dollar the cat got scared and Holly scooped him up in her arms.

Gary was *furious.* Not only was he furious, but he was embarrassed. His face was plastered with gooey ice cream, and his cheeks were red and his face was flushed. He got off his bike and let it fall to the ground. Terry and Larry got off their bikes.

"You guys really thought you were funny with that skunk trick," Larry said. "Well, I got news for you. Nobody pulls one over on us and gets away with it. *Nobody.*"

"And you won't get away with wrecking our clubhouse!" Dylan shouted, pointing his finger. "You guys are nothing but bullies!"

"That's right," Terry said. "And right now, we're

going to pound you guys into the ground!"

There was nothing we could do. The Martins wanted to fight, and there was no backing down now. I knew that we would lose, but we had to stand up to them.

"Ready Larry?" Gary asked, wiping the ice cream from his face.

"Ready," Larry replied.

"Terry?" Gary said.

"You bet," Terry replied. "Let's pound the little weasels!"

A bad day was about to get a lot worse.

17

Just as we were all preparing to defend ourselves, we heard a car come up behind us. The Martin brothers suddenly dropped their fists and began acting strange. Behind us, I could hear the car slow down. When I turned around, I suddenly understood why the Martins were acting so odd.

It was a police car. Not only was it a police car, but it was Officer Hulburt, a friend of ours. My dad and Officer Hulburt had gone to school together.

The squad car pulled up along next to us, and Officer Hulburt rolled down the window.

"Howdy, guys," he said.

"Hi," we all said. Except for the Martin brothers. They didn't like Officer Hulburt.

"How's the summer going?" he asked with a smile.

"Great," Dylan replied. "Except that the Martin brothers wrecked—"

Shane elbowed Dylan, urging him to be quiet.

"Yes?" Officer Hulburt said, eyeing the Martins suspiciously.

"Nothing," Dylan finished, looking at the ground.

"What he meant to say," Shane interjected, "is that Gary Martin wrecked his ice cream cone while he was riding his bike."

"Oh, that's too bad," Officer Hulburt said. "But it's a good thing he didn't fall and get hurt."

"Yeah, but they were just leaving, weren't you guys?" Lyle said.

Gary, Larry and Terry looked at Lyle, then at Officer Hulburt, then at one another.

"Yeah," Gary said in disgust. "We were just leaving. Come on, guys."

And with that, the three brothers hopped onto their bikes and rode off.

I sighed in relief. I think we all did. None of us wanted to get into a fight with the Martin brothers.

When they were gone, we explained everything that had happened to Officer Hulburt. We even told him about the skunk, and he laughed really hard.

But when we told him about our clubhouse, he was angry.

"The only problem, guys," he said to us, "is that you have no proof. If you have some kind of proof that the Martins destroyed your clubhouse, then I might be able to do something. If you can get some kind of evidence, then give me a call. I'll do anything I can for you."

He drove off, and the six of us stood on the shoulder of the road.

"Officer Hulburt is right," I said. "We still don't have any proof that the Martins were the ones that wrecked our clubhouse. Until we do, we might as well forget about it."

"I already have," Shane said. We all turned to look at him. He had a big smile on his face.

"What?!?!" Holly exclaimed.

"Yeah," Dylan echoed. "What are you talking about?"

"Guys . . . we can spend all summer being angry at the Martin brothers. We can plan revenge, we can waste a lot of time trying to prove that they destroyed our clubhouse. And what will that get us?"

We were silent, and Shane continued.

"I'll tell you what it will get us: a wasted summer. We still have a lot of time left before we go back to school. I don't want to waste a single day. I have an idea that I haven't told you guys about. Something that I've always wanted to do. It's really, really cool . . . and now is the perfect time to do it."

"What is it?" I asked.

"Yeah, what?" Holly repeated. She was still holding Dollar in her arms. The kitten had fallen asleep.

"Listen, guys," he began. "Listen to this . . . ."

And when he explained his idea, we all agreed: this was going to be one of the coolest projects the Adventure Club had ever done.

CLUBHOUSE CATASTROPHE

1

Shane's plan was to build the biggest, coolest clubhouse ever. Not just a single-room fort like the one we'd built on the other side of McArdle's farm, but a multi-level, four-room tree fort high in the air. He'd even drawn up a design on paper, and he showed it to us at a special Sunday meeting of the Adventure Club. Since our fort was destroyed, we all agreed to meet at the park behind the Great Bear Heart Library, which was right on the banks of Puckett Lake.

"You see," Shane said as he laid out his drawings on the picnic table. "If we're going to rebuild our clubhouse, we might as well go all-out. Let's make it the best in the world!”

And when he showed us his drawings, we gasped. The fort Shane had drawn was spectacular, with four separate rooms that connected. He’d really done a great job with his sketches, and it was obvious he’d already put a lot of time and thought into his plan.

“Shane!” Holly exclaimed. “That’s awesome!”

“Holy smokes!” Lyle said, then he let out a whistle. “How did you ever come up with that?”

“I read a book called *‘The Swiss Family Robinson’.”*

“I’ve read that!” Dylan proclaimed.

“You did not!” Tony disagreed. “You can’t read the back of a cereal box.”

“I did *too!”* Dylan insisted. “It’s about a family that lives in the forest, and they build a giant tree house!”

Shane nodded. “He’s right,” he said. “The family gets marooned on an island after a shipwreck. They’re forced to live there. It’s a great book, and ever since I read it, ’ e been thinking about how we could make a tree house like the Swiss Family Robinson.”

“But Shane,” Lyle said as he picked up one of Shane’s drawings, “this would cost a fortune.”

Shane shook his head. “I know we could round up the tools and all the nails we would need,” he said.

"Yeah," I said. "But the wood would cost a ton!"

"You're right, Parker," Shane said to me. "If we bought the wood at the lumber yard, it would cost us a lot more than we have. However—"

Shane paused and smiled, and we could tell that he had something up his sleeve.

"What?" Dylan prodded. "What are you thinking?"

"South of Devil's Ridge there's an old barn. It belongs to Mr. Beansworth. It's been there for years, and earlier this spring it started to collapse."

We nodded. All of us knew about Mr. Beansworth's old barn.

"Well, suppose we were allowed to use the wood from the barn to build our clubhouse?"

"You think we could *buy* the wood from Mr. Beansworth?" Tony asked.

Shane shook his head. "No, not buy," he said. "But what if the wood was free?"

"Free?!?!" Holly exclaimed. "Nobody is going to give away wood for free!"

Again, Shane nodded. "I already talked to Mr. Beansworth. Last night. He says we can have as much wood as we want, and that we'd be doing him a favor since he was going to pay someone to come out and dismantle what was left of the barn and haul away the wood."

"So, all that wood is ours?" I asked.

"If we want it," Shane said with a nod. "Of course, we all have to vote on it."

Our hands shot up in the air like lightning bolts.

"It's unanimous, then," Shane said. "As club president, I hereby declare our next project to be the construction of a new tree fort."

We cheered. Our new clubhouse was going to be the best ever built.

And we weren't going to waste another minute. We got started that very afternoon.

2

We all went home to gather up tools and other odds and ends that we would need. I borrowed my dad's hand saw and hammer, along with a leather tool apron that went around my waist. I also put on my hiking boots instead of my tennis shoes. Then I rode my bike along Great Bear Heart Mail Route road to a two-track trail that heads off to the right. Shane, Lyle, Tony, and Holly were already there. Holly was wearing a backpack, and Dollar the kitten was tucked in one of the pockets, his head and front two paws poking out.

A red wagon was tied to the back of Shane's bike. In it were boxes and boxes of nails of all shapes and sizes, a coiled rope, and a toolbox.

"I brought everything I thought we would need," he explained.

"Did anyone see the Martin brothers?" I asked.

Everyone shook their heads. It was important that the Martins didn't know what we were up to. There's no telling what they would do . . . and we couldn't risk having our new clubhouse demolished like our old one.

Fifteen minutes later, Dylan Bunker came riding up with his bike. He was panting and out of breath.

"Sorry I'm late, guys," he huffed.

"Let's get going," Tony said. "We have a lot of work ahead of us."

We rode our bikes along the trail. The day was sunny and hot, and soon, we had all worked up a sweat. After we passed the place where the trail leads out to Devil's Ridge, Shane called a halt.

"Let's rest here for a minute," he said.

We hopped off our bikes. Holly took off her backpack and let Dollar out. The kitten soon became infatuated with grasshoppers that hopped through the brush. It was kind of funny watching the tiny kitten trying to catch them.

"We're not far from Mr. Beansworth's old barn,"

Shane said, pointing. "It's on the other side of that hill over there."

Tony Gritter was the only one who had brought bottled water, and he passed it around. The water was cold and refreshing. We chatted excitedly about our project, and how cool it was going to be. We were so excited that no one realized that Lyle was missing, until Shane gave word to start off again.

"Hey," I said. "Where's Lyle?"

We all looked around.

"I didn't even know he was gone," Dylan said.

Shane cupped his hands around his mouth. "Lyle!" he shouted, his voice echoing through the forest. "Lyle! Where'dja go?!?!"

We waited. Soon, we could hear snapping twigs and branches. Lyle appeared through the trees.

"Right here," he said. He had big smile on his face.

"Where did you go?" I asked.

"Well, I think I solved our problem," he said.

"What problem?" Dylan asked.

"The biggest problem of all," Lyle replied. He was still grinning from ear to ear. "Wait until you see what I found."

We still didn't know what problem he was talking

about.

"Lyle," Shane said, "we've got everything we need."

Lyle shook his head. "Now we do, thanks to me," he said. "Come on."

Lyle turned and began walking back into the forest. The rest of us followed. Holly scooped up Dollar and carried the kitten in her arms.

"Lyle," Tony said. "Can't you give us a little clue?"

"In a minute," he said. "You'll see. Just a little farther."

We walked for another few minutes. Then Lyle stopped and looked at us. He was still smiling.

"So, we've got all the wood we need," Lyle said.

We all agreed. We had plenty of wood, thanks to Mr. Beansworth.

"And we have all of the tools we need," Lyle continued.

We all nodded.

"But there is still one thing we need," Lyle said. Then he was silent.

After a few moments, Dylan spoke. "We need a place to build it," he said quietly.

"Exactly!" Lyle shouted. "Dylan is right!"

"Wow," Shane said, scratching his head. "You're

right, Lyle. We need to find the perfect place."

"Not anymore," Lyle said. "Look up."

We all craned our necks back, looked up . . . and gasped.

3

Lyle Haywood had found a tree. Not just any tree, mind you . . . but the perfect tree for our new clubhouse.

Like the tree on the other side of McArdle's farm, it was a maple. The trunk was gigantic, and the tree was enormous.

What's more, about twenty feet off the ground, huge branches reached out like strong, muscular arms. The branches were bigger around than telephone poles, and we knew they'd be perfect to build the kind of tree house that Shane had designed.

"This is the one!" Tony exclaimed. "This place is perfect!"

"And it's far enough from the trail so that no one will see it," Lyle said. "Look at how thick the leaves are. We can build our fort up there and no one will ever see it!"

We were so excited we could hardly stand it.

We spent the rest of the day hauling lumber from Mr. Beansworth's barn. It was hard work. Some of the wood was rotted and couldn't be used, and we had to separate all of the good wood from the bad wood. All of the boards were faded and gray . . . and heavy. We worked through the afternoon, and by early evening, we were exhausted. Even little Dollar, who had followed us back and forth as we hauled the wood, was tired.

"Okay, I think we have enough lumber," Shane said as we stood and looked at the large pile of boards beneath the maple tree. We'd stacked the boards on top of each other, and the pile was as tall as we were.

"Let's get started!" Dylan suggested, but Shane shook his head.

"No," he said. "Not today. We're all too tired. We can't risk climbing this tree without all of our strength."

"Shane is right," Holly said. Dollar had fallen asleep in her arms, and Holly was gently stroking the kitten's ears. "It's too dangerous. One of us might slip and fall."

We decided that we would begin building the clubhouse first thing in the morning, right when the sun came up. We knew that we had a lot of work ahead of us, but we all wanted to finish the clubhouse as soon as possible.

Plus, we wanted to do a good job. We wanted to build the clubhouse to last a long time. We wanted to build something that we all would be proud of.

That night, I was so tired I think I fell asleep before my head even hit the pillow. But at midnight, I was awakened by a really bad dream. Have you ever had a nightmare where you can picture things, but it's really fuzzy and blurry? That's the kind of nightmare I had. I dreamed that the six of us in the Adventure Club were in our new clubhouse. I dreamed that we were having a meeting . . . but something horrible happened. Something that was unthinkable.

But I didn't know what it was. In my dream, we were all screaming and yelling in a panic. The nightmare was awful, and when I awoke, I was glad that I had only been dreaming.

I didn't know it at the time, of course, but that dream would soon come true.

4

We worked for three days straight—from sunup to sundown—to finish the clubhouse. The work was exhausting. Not only did we have to climb the tree, but we had to haul all of the wood up, too. That meant that we had to be extra-super-careful that we didn't fall.

But man . . . when we finished, we had the most incredible clubhouse anyone has ever seen. There were three main rooms, all connected by plank walkways with railings. Each room had open windows. We built a crude stairway from the main room that wound through the branches, and up to an open lookout platform. From there, we could see for miles and miles. And like our old clubhouse on the other side of McArdle's farm, we had a rope ladder that dangled down to the ground.

"But what if the Martin brothers discover our hideout?" Dylan asked. The six of us were standing at the bottom of the tree, looking up, admiring our work.

"I've already thought of that," Lyle replied. "Watch."

And with that, Lyle pulled out a small remote control from his pocket. "I got this at the thrift store," he said. "It belongs to a remote-control car."

"What good is that going to do?" I asked.

"Watch," Lyle said. He pointed the remote up at the clubhouse in the air, and pressed a button. Instantly, the rope ladder began to rise. Within seconds, it was too high for us to reach, and, after a minute, the rope had disappeared in the clubhouse.

"That's cool!" Holly exclaimed. "How did you do that?!?!"

"I just hooked up a small motor to the rope ladder," Lyle replied. "It works by remote control. Watch again."

Lyle pointed the remote again and pressed another button. Suddenly, the rope ladder began to come down.

"When we leave, all we have to do is use the remote control to raise the rope ladder," Lyle explained. "Plus, I also made a hand crank, so if the batteries in the remote or the motor run low, the rope can still be raised or lowered by hand."

"And if the Martin brothers happen to find our place, they won't be able to get to it!" Tony shouted. "That's great!"

"Well, they'll be able to get to it, if they really want to," Lyle explained. "But it will be really hard for them. This way, we'll prevent them from being able to climb up our rope ladder . . . simply because it will be rolled up in our clubhouse."

"Until we come back with the remote!" Dylan said. "This is too cool!"

And it was cool. I mean . . . I thought we had done a good job with our fort on the other side of McArdles's field . . . but this new clubhouse was even bigger and better. I couldn't wait until we held our very first meeting.

By this time, I had forgotten all about the nightmare I'd had earlier in the week. I'd forgotten how I'd awoke in the middle of the night, gripped by fear.

Besides . . . it was just a dream, that's all. Everybody has them. Nightmares don't come true.

But this one was about to.

BREGE '03

5

"The first meeting of the Adventure Club in our new clubhouse is now called to order," Shane said. We were all seated in a circle in the main room of our clubhouse. We didn't have any chairs or tables yet, but none of us cared. We were just happy to be in our new fort. It was raining, but we didn't care about that, either. The roof didn't leak like our old one, and that was great. A little rain blew through some of the open-air windows, but not enough to cause a problem.

Dollar the kitten seemed happy, too. He darted around the floor and followed the planks that led to the other rooms. Once in a while he would scurry out onto a limb to investigate. He sure was a fearless little cat.

"First order of business is to congratulate ourselves on finishing the clubhouse," Shane continued.

"Here, here!" we all said, and we raised our hands and slapped high-fives.

"Special commendation goes to Lyle for finding the perfect tree, and for creating the remote-control rope ladder. Anyone second the motion?"

"Seconded," said Holly, raising her hand.

"Done," Shane said with a nod. "Lyle Haywood, you are hereby acknowledged by members of the Adventure Club for outstanding service."

Lyle stood and bowed, and we all clapped and cheered. "Thank you," he said.

Thunder rumbled in the distance, and it began to rain harder. The wind whooshed through the trees, and our clubhouse swayed ever so gently.

"I also think that Mr. Beansworth should be formally thanked by all of us for his generous donation of wood."

"I second that," I said, raising my hand.

"Seconded by Parker Smith," Shane said. "Let's open a discussion on how Mr. Beansworth should be recognized."

We all talked about it, and, after a while, we decided

the best thing to do was to write a letter. Each of us would write a letter of thanks, and we would mail all six letters to Mr. Beansworth.

Lightning flashed, followed immediately by a loud peal of thunder. Dylan Bunker jumped, and Dollar the cat bounded into Holly's lap. All around us, branches moaned and groaned. The wind howled even louder.

"It sure is great to be in our new place," Tony said. "If it rained this hard in our old one, we'd be soaked."

"Speaking of soaked," Lyle said, "I have an idea about the *Independence.*"

The *Independence* was an old research submarine that we found in old man Franklin's junkyard. We got it working, but it sprang a leak and accidentally sank in Puckett Lake . . . with us inside it. We were lucky that nobody had been hurt.

"I don't even want to hear your idea, Lyle," Shane said. "Besides . . . it would probably take forever to find it. The *Independence* is long gone."

The submarine had been a sore subject. We spent a lot of time and money fixing the thing up, only to lose it. Shane Mitchell and Tony Gritter didn't want to waste any more time or money on the project; however, Holly, Dylan, Lyle and I have always wanted to go find it and salvage it. Shane and Tony said it would cost too much money, but the rest of us figured that we'd already spent a lot of money on it, and we might as well try and salvage the sub.

"I say we put it to a vote," Dylan said.

"I second that," Holly agreed.

Another flash of lightning lit up the sky, followed by an explosive burst of thunder. We hadn't realized it, but the sky had grown very, very dark, and it was only mid-afternoon.

"Man, it sure is storming out," I said, raising my voice above the shrieking wind.

"I'll go check it out," Tony said, getting to his feet.

"You're going to get soaked," Dylan said.

Tony shrugged. "So what's a little water?" He slipped out the back and climbed up the winding steps that led up to the lookout platform.

"As I was saying," Lyle continued, "I think we—" His voice was drowned out by the driving rain and howling wind . . . and the panicked shrieks of Tony Gritter. He came thundering down the steps, slipped on the last one, and fell headlong into the fort.

"TORNADO!" he screamed, scrambling to his knees. His face was flush red, his eyes brimming with terror.

"IT'S A TORNADO! IT'S HEADED RIGHT FOR US!"

6

In a split-second, we leapt to our feet and scrambled to the open-air window. Through the trees, we could see an ominous bank of dark, gray clouds. The rain was really coming down and the wind was blowing something terrible.

And then we saw it.

Above the trees, not far away at all, was a black finger of clouds, whirling and churning, spinning and whirring.

While we watched, we realized Tony was right: the tornado was headed right for us!

"We've got to get out of here!" Tony shrieked.

"Everybody out, now!" Shane ordered. "Hurry up!"

The rope ladder was still coiled around the mechanism that Lyle had designed. He pulled the remote from his pocket. At that exact moment, a surging gust of wind struck the clubhouse, causing it to rock violently, and throwing the six of us to the floor. The remote was knocked from Lyle's hand, bounced on a wood plank . . . and tumbled out the open trap door.

"Oh no!" Lyle screamed. He scrambled to the trap door in time to see the remote hit the ground below.

The tree was really whipping now, and the rain, swept by the intense gale, seemed to be falling sideways. It came through the open-air windows, soaking all of us.

"Now what?!?!" I shouted above the raging wind.

"We'll have to lower it by hand!" Lyle screamed. "Help me! We've got to hurry!"

I rushed to Lyle's side. The rope ladder was wound around a cylinder. Lyle began churning the hand crank as fast as he could. The rope ladder began to drop through the trap door.

I shot a glance behind me. Holly O'Mara was beneath the window, shielding her face from the rain. Dollar was tucked in the pocket of her sweatshirt. All you could see was the kitten's tail.

And outside, the menacing tornado kept coming. I could see debris flying through the air, being tossed in every direction.

I turned to help Lyle with the rope ladder. Tony was on his knees, helping Lyle turn the crank. Shane was pulling at the rope ladder, trying to make it go faster.

"The tornado is almost here!" Dylan cried. "It's coming right for us!"

"It's no use!" Lyle shouted. The roar of the approaching tornado was so loud that I could barely hear him. "There's no way we'll be able to lower the rope ladder in time!"

"Keep going!" Shane ordered. "We can't stop now!"

Somewhere, a branch snapped. Pieces of wood smacked against the side of the clubhouse. The tree moaned and groaned.

I turned and looked out the window, and screamed.

"Everybody hang on!" I wailed. *"Hang on tight! It's going to hit us!"*

7

There wasn't much to hang on to. With one hand, I grabbed Shane's ankle. With the other, I grabbed the edge of the trap door. Holly's arms were suddenly around my waist, and someone grasped my foot.

The thundering roar was deafening. The tree was really rocking now, whipping us back and forth, tossing us about. My knee banged into something, and I winced in pain.

The tree groaned. Branches snapped and broke as the hurricane force winds whipped at our helpless clubhouse. But it wasn't the clubhouse I was worried about. All I wanted to do was get through this alive—which, at the time, seemed very unlikely.

So much rain came through the open-air windows that the floor of our clubhouse flooded. There was nearly an inch of water on the floor. Leaves floated on the surface. Still, the tree whipped back and forth, hurling us helplessly around the room.

After nearly a full minute of complete terror, the wind began to subside. The rain seemed to lessen, and the tree wasn't rocking so violently anymore.

We were all heaving, gasping for breath. My heart thrashed. Holly released her grip around my waist and stuffed her hand into her pocket to make sure that Dollar was okay.

"Is . . . is it . . . gone?" Dylan stammered.

No one said a thing. We all sat in silence, listening to the water on the floor drain through the boards, listening to the wind blowing through the trees. We were soaked from head to toe, and water dripped from our chins and noses.

"I think we made it," Lyle finally said, adjusting his glasses with a single finger. "I think it passed by."

I couldn't believe how lucky we had been. The tornado had passed right over us . . . yet our clubhouse—and the big maple tree—was intact. We were safe.

Shane sat back and leaned against the wall. He raised his right hand.

"All in favor of never going through something like that again, say 'aye'."

We all raised our hands. "Aye," we echoed.

After we lowered the rope ladder, we climbed down. The ground was littered with broken branches, limbs, and leaves. We were all pretty lucky.

"I guess that proves we did a good job with the new clubhouse," Tony said. "I'm sure glad we built it right."

We didn't say much more. I think that we were all so freaked out about what had happened that we didn't know what to say. I, myself, was really grateful. I didn't want to think about what could have happened.

But there was one more thing we experienced on the way home. Something that was just as chilling as the experience we had just been through.

Something that made us really realize just how lucky we had been.

And when we passed McArdle's farm as we rode our bikes along Great Bear Heart Mail Route road, we saw something that none of us would ever, ever forget.

8

Holly O'Mara noticed it first, and she slowed her bike to a halt. She said nothing. I stopped my bike, and so did Lyle, Tony, Shane, and Dylan. We all turned to see what Holly was looking at.

On the far side of McArdle's farm, a large tree had been uprooted. It had been ripped violently from the ground and slammed to the earth. There were pieces of lumber strewn all over the field.

Pieces of lumber . . . from our old clubhouse. The tree that had been uprooted was the very same tree that we'd built our old clubhouse in. If we would have been in our old clubhouse when the tornado hit . . . .

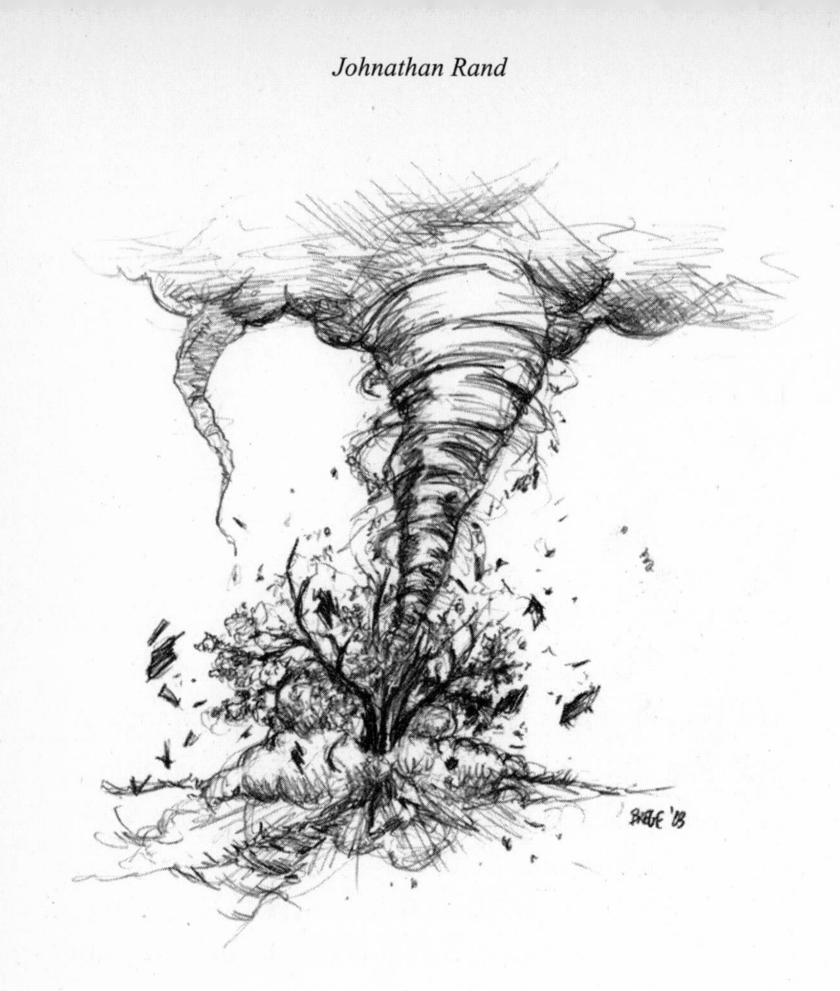

I couldn't bear to think about it.

For a long, long time, we sat in silence on our bicycles, looking at the fallen tree and the shattered lumber that used to be our fort. I thought about all of the fun we'd had in that clubhouse, and how hard we'd worked to build it.

I thought of the Martin brothers, and how they had wrecked it.

And I shivered. If the Martin brothers hadn't wrecked our clubhouse, we would still be using it. And there was a good chance that we would have been in it today.

When the tornado hit.

I gulped. I guess everything really *does* happen for a reason, just like my mom always says.

"Come on, guys," Shane said. "Let's go home."

The tornado was the talk of the town. The terrible storm had gone north of Great Bear Heart, so there wasn't much damage in the village itself, but there were a lot of branches and limbs all over the place. Our parents had been worried sick about us, but, thankfully, none of us got into any trouble. How could we? I mean . . . we hadn't done anything wrong. I got a lecture from Dad about how it's important to make sure that he and Mom knew where I was (which they did, because I told them where I was going earlier that day). But he wasn't mad, which was cool. He suggested that we take a radio out to our clubhouse, so we could get weather reports and know if any storms were coming. That was a good idea. I sure didn't want to go through that tornado experience again!

The next meeting of the Adventure Club was scheduled for three days later. I was just about ready to hop on my bike and head out to our new clubhouse when the phone rang. It was Lyle.

"Hey, I've rescheduled our meeting place," he said. "We're not going to meet at the new clubhouse."

"How come?" I replied.

"You'll see. Just be at the park in ten minutes."

I hung up, hopped on my bike and rode to the park. Dylan was already there, which was surprising. He's usually always late. Just as I got there, Holly rode up on her bike, followed by Shane. Then Tony arrived.

"Where's Lyle?" Shane asked. "And why did he want to meet here at the park?"

Holly smiled. "I know," she smirked.

"Tell us," Dylan said.

Holly shook her head. "Not yet. Not until Lyle gets here."

In a few minutes, Lyle arrived. A pair of binoculars dangled from his neck.

"Hey gang," he said, skidding his bike to a halt.

"Sorry about the change in plans. I just wanted everybody to see something."

We were all seated at a picnic table near the water, and he walked over to us and sat down. Then he removed his glasses and raised the binoculars to his eyes. He moved them sideways, back and forth, scanning the lake, until finally—

"There it is. Have a look." He removed the binoculars from around his neck and handed them to Shane. Shane raised them to his face.

"What am I supposed to be looking for?" he asked. "All I can see is water. And a tiny white buoy."

"It's not a buoy, it's an empty plastic milk jug," Lyle said. "And that's exactly what you're supposed to see."

"Huh?" Shane said, handing the binoculars to Tony. Tony pressed the binoculars to his face.

"Okay," he said. "I see it. Big deal."

Dylan was next, then the binoculars were handed to me. I had no problem finding the tiny white speck in the lake. Actually, if you looked carefully, you could see it without binoculars.

"You brought us here to show us a plastic milk jug?" Shane said, rolling his eyes.

Lyle smiled, and so did Holly.

"Yes," Lyle said. "Holly and I rowed out there yesterday. I used the gallon jug to mark the spot."

Dylan's eyes just about popped out of his head. "Is it a good fishing spot?" he inquired.

"Well, I don't know about that," Lyle said. "But one end of that rope is attached to the gallon jug. The other end of the rope is attached to a brick, so we could mark the spot."

"Come on, come on . . . what spot?" Shane said impatiently.

Lyle looked at Holly. Both were grinning. Holly spoke.

"Twenty feet below that buoy is a brick," she began. "Right next to that brick . . . is the *Independence.*"

"We rowed out yesterday and searched for it," Lyle continued. "You can actually see the shape of the sub from the surface. Holly even dived down just to be sure."

"It's the *Independence,* all right," she said, nodding.

So we took a vote. Tony and Shane still thought that trying to raise the sub and fix it back up would cost a lot of money, but, in the end, they voted in favor of salvaging the vessel.

And that was that. The six of us voted that we

would, somehow, retrieve the sub from where it lay. We would somehow bring it to shore and fix it up, and use it to explore the bottom of Puckett Lake.

And I'll say this much: hang on. Because what was about to happen was one of the most exciting adventures of the summer.

RAISING THE INDEPENDENCE

1

We all knew what we were up against.

Just because we knew where the crippled submarine was, didn't mean that the rest of our job would be any easier. Somehow, we had to find a way not only to bring the sub to the surface, but also to get it to shore. The task wasn't going to be easy.

Which was okay with us. We knew that if we put our heads together and made good plans, we could do just about anything. We knew that it would be complicated, but that was part of the fun.

The six of us were seated on overturned milk crates in the main room of our new clubhouse, sipping root beers. Tony Gritter had gone to the Great Bear Heart Market, and George Bloomer, the owner, had given him six old milk crates for us to use as chairs, since our other ones had been demolished. Mr. Bloomer is really cool. When we set up a stand to sell food earlier in the summer, he sold us materials and food at a discount so we could make money.

"I say we get a big, strong boat, and hook a chain to it," Dylan Bunker said. "We can drag the *Independence* to shore!"

"There's no way that will work, Dylan," Shane said. "The *Independence* is way too heavy."

"We need to figure out a way to lift the sub up," Lyle suggested. "If we can bring it up to the surface, then we could tow it in to my dad's boathouse."

That's where we'd originally fixed up the sub when we brought it over from Franklin's junkyard. Lyle's dad has a boathouse right on the water that he doesn't use anymore. It was the perfect place to store the sub—that is, of course, until it sank when it sprang a leak.

We sat around for over an hour, coming up with various ideas how we could salvage the submarine. Holly started writing down different ideas that we came up with. All of them seemed impossible, or would cost too much money.

And that was our *other* problem. We didn't have much money, so however we salvaged the *Independence,* we'd have to do it on a shoestring budget.

After a while, I noticed that Shane hadn't said anything. He was slowly scratching his chin, staring out the open-air window, looking up into the tree.

"Wait a second, wait a second," he finally said. His eyes were shining, and he smiled as he looked at each one of us. He spoke carefully, cautiously. "I saw a movie once, about a ship that sank. There was this team of researchers that wanted to raise it from the bottom of the ocean. And they did."

"How did they do it?" I asked.

"Balloons!" Shane exclaimed, spreading his arms wide. "They used giant balloons, called 'lift bags'! What they did was take the balloons, unfilled, to the bottom of the ocean. Then they fastened them to the ship."

"But how would that work?" Dylan asked. "I mean . . . if the balloons didn't have any air in them, they wouldn't rise to the surface or anything."

"They pumped air from the surface through a hose that went to the bottom of the ocean," Shane explained. "That's how they filled the lift bags. When the balloons began to fill with air, they began to rise—"

"Lifting the ship with it!" Tony finished.

"Yep!" Shane said.

"How big were the balloons?" Lyle asked as he adjusted his glasses.

"Huge," Shane replied. "Bigger than a truck."

"Where are we going to get balloons like that?" Holly asked. Dollar the cat had been roaming around the clubhouse, and now the creature leapt onto Holly's lap. She scratched the kitten's head and it immediately began to purr.

"We won't need balloons that big," Shane said. "We would just need four big bags that could hold air."

"Garbage bags!" Dylan cried.

Lyle shook his head. "You're on the right track," he said thoughtfully. "But garbage bags wouldn't be strong enough. We need something that won't fall apart under the weight of the sub."

Once again, we all started chattering and talking. We came up with a lot of good ideas, but so far, we couldn't think of a single thing that we could use as a lift bag.

Tony took a sip from his bottle of root beer. Then he held the bottle up and stared at it. He frowned as if he was deep in thought.

"What's the matter, Tony?" Holly smirked. "Never seen a bottle before?"

"That's it!" Tony said, ignoring Holly's comment. "They would be perfect!"

"Bottles?" Shane said with a frown.

"No!" Tony said. "Think about it!"

We all sat and looked at Tony and his bottle of root beer, but we couldn't figure out what he meant.

"All right," Tony finally said after we couldn't figure out what he was talking about. "I'll show you. Come on."

As we followed Tony out of the clubhouse, down the rope ladder, and rode our bikes into town, none of us had a clue what he had in mind—but when we understood what he had been thinking about, we all knew that his idea was *perfect*.

2

We followed Tony until he stopped right in front of the Great Bear Heart Market. The store was busy, with a few cars sitting in front of the gas pumps and shoppers buying groceries. Across the street, in Puckett Park, kids played on the beach and frolicked in the water.

Tony hopped off his bike and took off his backpack. Inside was his empty bottle of root beer.

"Watch," he said, and he walked over to a box as big as he was. The giant box was used for returnables—bottles and cans that were to be recycled. While we watched, Tony deposited the bottle in the box, then walked back to where the five of us were standing.

"I still don't get it," Dylan said.

"Come on, guys!" Tony said, tapping his temple with his index finger. "Can't you figure it out?"

"I just did!" Lyle exclaimed. "Tony . . . you're a genius!"

"Well, that too," Tony smirked.

"The bags used to store the returned bottles and cans!" Lyle said. "The bag lines the inside of the box! They're five times bigger than ordinary garbage bags—"

"—and they're super-strong!" Tony interjected.

They were right!

We ran up to the box. It was filled with bottles and cans . . . but, more important, there was a thick, milky-colored plastic bag that lined the box!

"This will do it!" Lyle explained, fingering the material. "The bag is big, so it will hold a lot of air. And it's made of really thick plastic, so it's super strong!"

We asked the market owner, Mr. Bloomer, if we could borrow four bags. When we told him what we wanted them for, he just laughed.

"You crazy kids in the Adventure Club," he said, smiling and shaking his head. "You're always up to something."

Mr. Bloomer loaned us four bags.

The rest of the project took on a life of its own. Holly O'Mara has an older brother who is a scuba diver, so we borrowed one of his air tanks. Lyle fitted a garden hose to the tank. The other end of the hose would be inserted in the lift bags when we had them fastened to the subs. Then, from the surface, we would open the valve on the air tank. Air would be forced down the hose and out the other end. The bubbles would rise . . . filling the bag with air. Which, of course, would cause the bags to rise to the surface . . . bringing the *Independence* with them.

Dylan Bunker's mom and dad agreed to let us borrow their pontoon boat, which was big enough for all six of us. We could use the boat to pull the *Independence* to the shore once we got it up from the bottom of the lake.

By the end of the day, we had everything prepared. It was too late to do much more, since it was getting dark. Instead, we built a fire down by the water and toasted marshmallows. We were all circled around the fire, our faces reflecting the flickering orange and yellow flames. The fire popped and cracked, and crickets chirred in the shadows around us. Dollar had caught a large bug and was batting it around with his paws.

"Man, I can't wait until we fix that sub!" Dylan exclaimed, popping another marshmallow into his mouth. "Thaphs gumma be awthum!"

"Are we going to find that underwater tunnel again?" I asked. Before the sub sank, we had located a tunnel that went all the way out to Lake Huron. Problem was, when we'd surfaced, we'd almost hit a huge freighter!

"I don't know," Lyle replied. "That was kind of dangerous. I think there's a lot of stuff we could explore right here in Puckett Lake."

Nobody knew for sure what we were in for, and that made the whole adventure even more exciting . . . an adventure that was only one day away.

3

We met at the park the next morning. From there, we walked down to the lake where the Bunker's kept their pontoon boat. The sun was just coming up on the other side of the lake. A few early morning fishermen were out. A pair of loons moved slowly through the water, disappearing now and then as they dove for fish. Seagulls sat on docks, all puffed up and feathery, still groggy from sleep.

Shane and Holly had put together a list of things we would need, and we checked and re-checked to make sure we had everything.

"Tank and hose?" Holly called out, reading from a

clipboard.

"Check," I said.

"Ropes and cables?" Holly said.

"Got'em," Dylan replied.

"Lift bags?"

"All four of 'em, right here," Lyle said.

"Life jackets?"

I counted the orange vests piled at the front of the boat.

"Six of them," I said.

"Tools?"

"Yep," Lyle answered.

"Dollar?" Holly called out.

"Right here," I said, picking up the kitten that was at my feet. I handed him to Holly, and she took the cat with one arm.

"And Tony and I have our masks and fins," Shane said.

"Let's go!" Dylan exclaimed, and he leapt to the wheel. With the turn of a key the engine roared to life. The rest of us scrambled for our seats, and Dylan expertly backed the pontoon boat away from the dock.

We were on our way.

It only took us about five minutes to reach the white

jug that was the buoy marker for the *Independence.* Sure enough, when we looked down, we could see the dark shadow of the submarine below.

Dylan cut the engine and tossed out the anchor.

"Okay, guys," Shane ordered. "Let's get busy. We've got a lot of work to do."

It took us a couple of hours to prepare the bags. Lyle and Shane had devised a special cable harness that would attach to the sub. Two lift bags would be affixed to the front, and two on the back.

Shane and Tony would have the job of filling the bags. Using their masks and fins, they would have to swim down and stick the hose into each empty bag.

"The trick," Lyle explained, "is to fill a little bit of air into each bag. If one bag gets filled with too much air, the sub will be unbalanced, and it might roll over while we're towing it to the boathouse."

"Let's do it!" Tony exclaimed, and he and Shane got busy donning their masks and fins. They leapt fins first into the water, then surfaced a moment later.

Holly and I handed Shane two of the lift bags and the harness. Dylan handed the other two bags and harness to Tony. The two divers gave each other the 'okay' sign—making a circle by touching the index finger to the thumb—and disappeared beneath the surface.

They were gone for nearly a minute. Shane and Tony are both very good swimmers, and they can hold their breath for a long time.

Shane was the first to surface. "Got it!" he said, swimming to the boat and clinging to the ladder. "That was easy."

Tony surfaced next. "Ready for the hose," he said. "This is going to be a piece of cake."

"How's the sub look?" Lyle asked.

"Pretty good," Tony said, raising his face mask to his forehead. "There's some green film on the window, and the whole sub is covered with a thin layer of silt. But it doesn't look bad at all."

"That'll clean up easy," said Lyle. "Our main problem, after we get it back to the boathouse, is to find and repair the leak."

Now the real work was about to begin. Lyle opened the air valve and placed his thumb on the end of the hose.

"Keep your thumb over it until you're ready to let the air out," he explained. "Otherwise, we'll run out of air before the bags are filled."

Shane and Tony took turns diving down with the

hose, careful to fill a small amount into each bag. After half an hour, they'd only filled the bags halfway.

"I've got to rest," Shane said, swimming to the pontoon boat. Lyle and I helped him up the ladder. Tony, too, decided to take a break. All that swimming—up, down, up, down—was really tiring.

Dylan opened up the boat's cooler.

"Surprise," he said.

We looked inside. There were six cans of lemonade, and six wrapped sandwiches.

"I made them myself!" he said, proudly holding up a sandwich. "One for each of us."

Now, I've got to say this: Dylan can be kind of klutzy, but he's got to be one of the most unselfish, kindest people I know. It was really thoughtful of him to go to all that work and make us each a sandwich for the day.

But the sandwiches were *terrible!* I mean . . . they were *awful!* The sandwich Dylan gave me was tuna fish and honey! Blechhh! I thought I was going to puke! Holly's sandwich looked like it was peanut butter and mayonnaise. I could tell by the look on her face when she bit into it that it must have tasted just as bad as mine. Lyle almost gagged when he took a bite of his.

"How are they?" Dylan said as he took a big bite of his sandwich.

"Great," I fibbed.

"Yeah, terrific," Holly echoed. She forced herself to swallow, and she looked pale.

We all ate our sandwiches, suffering through every miserable bite. Holly tried to give Dollar a tiny bite, and I thought the cat was going to jump overboard.

And not one of us complained to Dylan. Sure, the sandwiches were awful, and could have made us sick. But, most importantly, Dylan had taken it upon himself to do something really nice for all of us. He did it on his own, without being asked.

We need more people like Dylan Bunker in this world.

And besides: he'd used his own money to buy the lemonades . . . which we all gulped down quickly. Not necessarily because we all liked lemonade . . . but we were all eager to wash down the terrible taste of the sandwiches.

Then we just kind of hung out for a while. Tony and Shane wanted to wait for their food to digest before they went swimming (or maybe they were just waiting to see if the sandwiches they ate were going to kill them). We talked about how much fun we were going to have when we fixed up the *Independence.*

An hour later, Tony and Shane were back in the water. Up, down, up, down. Each took turns filling the bags with air.

"They're almost filled," Tony said, gasping for breath when he broke the surface. "A couple more shots of air is going to do it, I think."

Shane took the hose from Tony.

"Be careful," Lyle warned. "If something happens while the sub starts to rise and you're beneath it—"

He didn't have to finish his sentence. We all knew that we'd reached the most dangerous part of the project.

Tony tread water. "I'll stay right here, watching you from the surface, just in case something goes wrong," he said.

Shane took a deep breath.

Tony spoke again. "Shane . . . be careful, man."

Shane looked up at us, then looked at Tony, nodded, and slipped beneath the surface with the hose.

"   , I hope he's careful," Dylan said quietly.

We waited in silence. Shane seemed to be gone forever. Finally, after nearly a minute, Lyle spoke, his voice tense with alarm.

"Something's wrong," he said. "Shane's been gone too long."

"Tony! What do you see?!?!" I asked loudly.

Tony was only a few feet away, treading water. He was staring down through his face mask. He turned to us.

"I can't see much," he replied. Since his nose was covered by his dive mask, his voice sounded congested, like he had a cold.

"Do you see Shane?" Holly asked worriedly.

"No," Tony called back.

"He's been down there too long," Lyle repeated. "Something's wrong. Something's really, really wrong."

Without another word, Lyle frantically kicked off his shoes and dove into the water. Dylan did the same, followed by me, then Holly.

Up until then, we'd all been concerned about the sub and getting it to the boathouse.

Now, our plans had changed. Now, we were in a race against time to save our club president, Shane Mitchell.

4

As soon as I opened my eyes underwater, I saw a fuzzy sight that I'll never forget:

The *Independence.*

Buoyed by the four air bags, the submarine was gently rising to the surface! Shane held onto one of the bags, slowly gliding with the vessel as it rose! It was an incredible sight. Relief flowed through my body as I realized that Shane was okay.

I watched until I ran out of breath, then I surfaced and swam to the boat. Holly had already climbed back up, and her sopped clothing was clinging to her skin. She helped me onto the boat, and I helped Lyle and Dylan up.

Still, something puzzled me. Shane still hadn't surfaced. He'd been underwater now for over two minutes. Two whole minutes! That's a long time to hold your breath.

Tony stayed on the surface, looking down through his mask.

"Here she comes!" he shouted as he looked up. "She's coming up!"

The four cream-colored lift bags slowly appeared, rising like ghosts. They looked like four giant eggs beneath the surface.

"Can you see Shane?" I asked Tony.

"Yeah, he's fine," Tony replied.

Three minutes had gone by. Shane had been under water for three minutes. It seemed impossible.

Suddenly, the four lift bags were at the surface, just barely breaking the top of the water. Several feet beneath the balloons we could see the looming shape of the *Independence,* suspended in the water by the air-filled balloons.

Still, there was no sign of Shane. Tony swam casually to the side of the boat. Dylan and I helped him aboard.

"Where's Shane?" Holly asked.

Tony pointed. "He's fine," he said. "I mean . . . he sure didn't look like he was having any trouble."

Another tense minute ticked by before Shane finally appeared. We all heaved a sigh of relief as he swam up to the pontoon boat.

"Man, you held your breath for over four minutes!" I exclaimed. "How did you *do* that?"

Shane scrambled aboard, still holding the hose. "Simple," he replied, raising the end of the hose to his mouth. He released his thumb, and air hissed out. "I just used the air coming from the hose to breathe," he said.

So that was it! He hadn't held his breath, after all! He'd used the air from the hose, instead of coming to the surface for air!

"The bags were really unbalanced, and I knew that if I took the time to surface, the sub might flip," he said. "It just made more sense to take a breath from the hose and continue working to make sure each lift bag was filled with equal amounts of air."

Now *that* was brilliant. You can see why we elected Shane Mitchell as president of the Adventure Club.

Getting the vessel back to the boathouse turned out

to be a lot harder than we thought. Tony dived down, attached a cable to the front of the sub, and hooked the other end of the cable to the pontoon boat.

The problem was this: the *Independence* was so heavy that, even with the pontoon's motor raging at full throttle, the sub and the boat crept along at a snail's pace. It was like towing a glacier. It took us the entire afternoon to make it back, then it took us the rest of the evening to hoist it into the boathouse with winches and pulleys. Finally, as night began to settle in, the *Independence* rested on blocks and boards in the boathouse. All of the water d drained out from her (including a few fish that had found their way inside).

"I want to start working on her right now," Lyle said as he sat on the dock next to the sub. "But I'm so tired, I think I could fall asleep right here."

"Me too," Dylan said, collapsing on the dock.

"Everyone in favor of meeting here tomorrow morning at eight, raise your hand," Shane said, showing us his palm.

The five of us responded by raising our hands at the same time.

"Motion passed," Shane said tiredly.

Holly looked at Dylan. "Dylan," she began, "that

was so nice of you to make those sandwiches today," she said.

"Want me to make more for tomorrow?" Dylan replied, eager to please. His eyes were wide, and he glanced at each of us.

"No, I wouldn't want you to go through all that work again," Holly said. "Besides . . . I'd like to make sandwiches for tomorrow."

Tony piped up in the nick of time. "All in favor of Holly making the sandwiches, raise their hand."

We couldn't get our hands in the air fast enough.

5

The next day was dark and gloomy. A steady rain fell, creating large puddles and winding bands of water that snaked their way to the lake. Normally, it would have been a day to stay indoors and play a game or something.

Not today.

I was too excited. I wanted to get to work on the *Independence* right away. All of us did. I didn't care if it stormed all day. By the time we reached the boathouse we were soaked, but none one complained. Besides . . . we'd be in and out of the water while we worked, so the rain really didn't bother us at all.

When I arrived at the boathouse, Lyle Haywood was

already there. He'd unlocked the big door and was already inspecting the sub.

"Hi Parker," he said, glancing up as I walked inside.

"How's it going?" I replied.

"Cool," he said. Then he slowly shook his head. "We have a lot of work to do on this thing."

"Did you find the leak?" I asked.

"Yeah. That won't be too hard to fix, I don't think. But everything else is waterlogged. All of the electronics, all the lights and the battery are ruined. They'll all have to be replaced."

"Can't we get a lot of that stuff from the junkyard?" When we'd restored the submarine the first time, we were able to use a lot of odds and ends that we found at Franklin's old dump on the other side of town.

"Yeah, mostly," he said. "But some of the things we'll have to buy."

Just then, Shane strode in, followed by Tony.

"How's she look?" Shane asked Lyle.

"I was just telling Parker that we have a lot of work to do," Lyle answered.

"Then let's get started!" Tony said. "I can't wait to take her out again!"

Dylan strolled in. Holly followed about ten minutes

later. She was carrying a brown sack. Dollar the kitten was scampering around her ankles. Even the cat seemed excited.

"Sandwiches for lunch," Holly said, setting the bag in the corner of the boathouse.

And we got to work. Lyle made a list of things we were going to need, and the items filled two pages. Dylan and I volunteered to hike over to the junkyard to see what we could find. Old man Franklin let us have anything we wanted for free, which was really great, because there were a lot of things we'd need to get. Lyle had listed things like a car radio, light bulbs from the tail lights of cars, wires, sheet metal . . . all sorts of things. It took us three trips just to haul all of the materials to the boathouse.

Around noon, we took a break and ate the sandwiches Holly had brought. They were ten times better than the ones Dylan had made!

Then it was back to work.

Tony repaired the hull by welding the spot where the sub had sprang a leak. Lyle and Shane got to work re-wiring the vessel and replacing the electronics. Holly worked at cleaning the entire sub from top to bottom. She scrubbed and scrubbed until the metal gleamed like new.

All of this, of course, didn't happen in one day. It took us over a week to get the *Independence* ready. Plus, all of us had to chip in to pay for things that we needed. I made ten dollars mowing Lucy Marbles' yard, and I had to use the money to buy eight small light bulbs. Finally, Lyle announced that the wiring was complete.

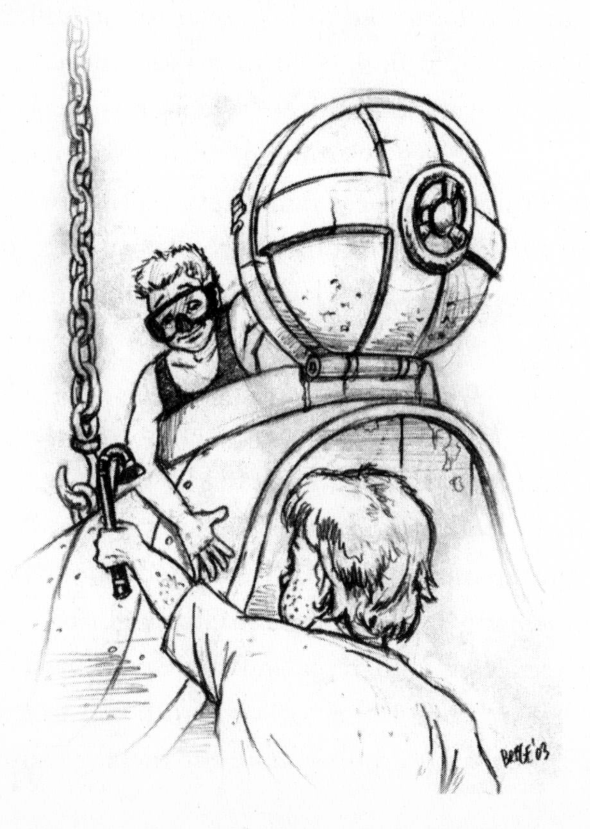

"Let's power up," he said.

"Are we going to take it out now?" Dylan asked. We were all standing around the sub, which was still hoisted up in the boathouse.

"Not just yet," Lyle replied. "Let's make sure everything works."

He scrambled into the sub, and a moment later he re-appeared through the thick viewing glass at the front.

"Okay," he said. His voice sounded oddly hollow from inside the sub. "We'll try the lights first."

He flicked a switch. Suddenly, two bright beams appeared from each side of the sub. These were the spotlights, which were actually the headlights from an old van we found in Franklin's junkyard.

Shane gave Lyle the 'thumbs up' sign. "Spotlights are a go," he said.

"Interior," Lyle said, flicking another switch. Instantly, the lights on the inside of the sub flickered on.

"Cool," Lyle said. "And the system." He flicked a switch, and the lights died. For a moment, we thought that something wasn't working right.

All of a sudden, there was a loud hum. I could see the control panel lights on the inside of the sub glowing.

"Perfect!" Lyle said. "Everything's got power!"

"Now can we take it out?" Dylan asked again.

"Not until we know for sure that it doesn't leak," Lyle said. "We have to make sure that our patch job worked."

It took all six of us to use the winch and lower the sub into the water. Lyle closed the main hatch, and we lowered the submarine until it was completely under water.

"Now we wait a while," Shane said. "Let's meet back here in two hours."

I couldn't believe it. I had thought that the *Independence* was gone for good. Now we had found and restored it for the second time.

And I wasn't worried. The last time, we'd been a little careless, and had gotten into some serious trouble.

Not this time, though. I knew that this time we would be extra careful. We would take every precaution to make sure that we'd be safe.

And I tried to imagine what we would see while exploring the bottom of Puckett Lake. Last time, we'd spotted a big sturgeon, which was really cool, and a big northern pike. I was sure we'd see more fish.

Which we would, of course. Puckett Lake was filled with all different kinds of fish.

But we would also find something else—something I would have never imagined to find in a million years.

6

Two hours seemed like two years.

My arms were covered with grease and dirt, and my shoes were caked with mud, so I went home and took a shower. Dad grilled hamburgers for dinner, and I ate two of them. All the while, I kept looking at the clock. I couldn't wait to take the *Independence* on another voyage.

Finally, it was time. I rode my bike to the boathouse, only to find I was the last one to arrive.

"Parker's here!" Dylan exclaimed. He jumped up and down. *"Yes! Yes! Yes!"* he exclaimed. *"We're taking her out!"*

The top of the sub was above the surface, and the

main hatch was open. Lyle and Shane had already inspected the vessel for leaks.

"Dry as a bone inside," Shane told me.

Lyle was the first to climb inside, followed by Holly, then Dylan, then Tony, me, and finally, Shane. He closed the hatch behind him.

Inside the sub was so cool! We were a little cramped, but nobody cared. Lyle took his seat at the helm, since he was the one who knew the most about the sub, and had piloted the vessel the last time we had taken it out.

At the front of the sub was a big viewing window. Even sitting next to the dock in about six feet of water, it was kind of cool. Like looking into a murky aquarium.

Lyle flicked a switch. Lights on the control panel blinked on, and the motor started up.

"Everybody ready?" Lyle asked.

"Yeah," we all replied.

Lyle placed his hand on the control lever and pushed it forward. The sub lurched to the side, then slid ahead. It bumped into one of the dock pilings, then Lyle made an adjustment and moved the sub away from the dock. A small bluegill appeared directly in front of us. It looked at us curiously, as if it was wondering just what kind of fish we were. Then it darted off.

"Where are we heading?" I asked.

"Shane and I looked at a map of the lake a little while ago," Lyle replied. "There's a really deep part to the southeast of here."

"How deep?" Dylan asked.

"About a hundred and twenty feet," Shane replied.

I whistled. *A hundred and twenty feet?!?!?* I thought.

Too cool.

The submarine slipped easily through the water. Soon, the surface disappeared, and we knew we were in deeper water.

"How deep are we?" Holly asked.

Lyle looked at the control panel. "Thirty-six feet," he replied. "The deeper we go, the darker it will be."

We traveled in silence. The only thing we heard was the hum of the motor as the *Independence* slid through the water. We saw a smallmouth bass pass right in front of us, but it wasn't very big.

"Maybe we'll see another sturgeon!" Holly said, after the bass vanished.

"We'll have to keep our eyes peeled," Lyle said.

The sub stayed right near the bottom. There wasn't too much to see . . . just a lot of weeds and logs. Some of the logs were huge, though. Years ago, much of the area around Great Bear Heart was lumbered. The wood was transported to the lake and through the inland waterway, where it was loaded onto large trailers and hauled away to the mill.

And Lyle was right. The deeper we went, the darker it became.

"Captain Mitchell?" Lyle said.

"Yes, Captain Haywood?" Shane replied, very official-like.

"Spotlight, please."

"Aye, aye, sir," Shane replied. He reached over his shoulder and flicked a switch. Instantly, a bright beam of light lit up the area in front of the submarine.

But it also lit up something else . . . and when we saw it, we gasped in amazement.

7

It was a muskellunge.

Now, if you've never seen a muskellunge before, just try to imagine the meanest, scariest fish in the world. A muskellunge looks a lot like a barracuda, only meaner. The last time we had the *Independence* under sail, we saw a northern pike, which is closely related to the muskellunge. They look a lot alike, except for their coloring.

And the one that was in front of our sub was *huge.* In Puckett Lake, muskellunge will grow to nearly five feet in length . . . sometimes even bigger. They have rows of razor-sharp teeth, and their body is long and narrow, like a big, fat tube. They are a really ferocious fish, and if you ever catch one, you have to be careful so you don't get bit. My dad said that when he was a boy, he caught a muskellunge. When he tried to remove the hook from its mouth, the fish bit his hand. Dad needed twenty stitches to sew up the wound.

"It's a monster!" Dylan exclaimed.

"It's a muskie!" Shane said, calling the fish by its popular nickname. "That thing is gigantic! It's the biggest one I've ever seen!"

Lyle, who loves to fish, piped up. "Man, where's my fishing rod when I need it?"

We all laughed. The thought of using a fishing rod in a submarine seemed kind of funny.

The muskellunge swam right up to the sub. It wasn't afraid of us at all. It turned sideways and eyeballed us, and I was wondering if he was looking at us like we might be a tasty snack. Thankfully, muskies don't eat people, but the sight of the giant fish that filled our entire viewing window was a little unnerving. The fish was easily as long as Dylan was tall.

After a few moments of inspection, the muskie swam off into the murky darkness.

"That was awesome!" Holly gasped.

"Captain Gritter?" Lyle said.

"Yes, sir?" Tony replied.

"You're in charge of the light. Sweep it back and forth in front of us."

Tony did as he was ordered. The movement of the light was controlled by a small joystick on the side of the submarine. The motion of the light was powered by a small electric motor that we'd taken from a car. Originally, the motor had been used to control the car's side-view mirrors. It worked perfect as a remote control for our spotlight.

"One hundred feet," Lyle said. The sub churned on, slowly slinking through the depths. No one said a thing.

"One hundred twenty feet," Lyle finally said. "We're here. The deepest part of Puckett Lake."

Tony swept the spotlight around. It was really, really dark. Without the light, it would be really hard to see anything.

Here, at the very deepest part of Puckett Lake, it looked like we were seeing some kind of strange, underwater desert. The bottom was sandy. A few rocks, none of them bigger than a softball, were scattered about. Some plants grew, and most of those were small, too. A large log had settled in the muck, and only the top of it was visible. It was obvious that it had been there for a long time.

And suddenly, the light fell upon something that we'd never expected to find.

Something that shouldn't have been at the bottom of the lake.

And that changed our entire adventure, right then and there.

8

"What in the world is *that?!?!*" Dylan exclaimed.

A large object had suddenly appeared in the light. In fact, if we hadn't seen it at that moment, we would have probably ran into it. Lyle slowed the sub, and we hovered, motionless, a few feet off the bottom.

I know this is going to sound strange . . . but what we were looking at appeared to be a small gasoline pump. Clumps of zebra mussels clung to it. Zebra mussels are small clams, about the size of your thumbnail, and they cluster together in tight groups. The object was caked with slime and mud, and it stood upright. Whatever it was, I was sure it was man-made.

"It looks like a gas pump," I said.

"Yeah," Tony snickered. "Why don't you pull up alongside and we'll top off the tank."

"No, no," Lyle said cautiously. "That's not a gasoline pump. It's too small. Let's get a little closer."

Lyle expertly guided the *Independence* right up to the object. We were now only inches away.

"Do you think it's something from a boat?" Holly asked.

Shane shook his head. "I don't know," he said. "Captain Haywood?"

Lyle shook his head. "It's hard to tell," he said. "It's been at the bottom of the lake for so long that it's covered with gunk. It almost looks like a large bubble gum machine."

"Anybody got a quarter?" Tony said with a chuckle.

"Eeewww," Holly said. "That would be some pretty awful gum!" We all laughed.

"With all of that gunk all over it, it's hard to tell what it might be, Shane said. Captain O'Mara . . . draw a sketch on a piece of paper."

Holly pulled out her notepad from her back pocket and quickly drew a small sketch of what she saw. "How's that?" she said, holding it up for all of us to see.

"Perfect," Lyle said. Then he looked back at the object resting on the bottom of the lake. "Man . . . that's really weird. I'll see if I can go around it to get a look at it from the other side." He pulled the lever back, then pressed a couple of buttons. The engine slowed, then there was a loud clunk that gave us all a start. Lyle chuckled. "Just putting her in reverse," he said.

The *Independence* slowly backed up. Then Lyle shifted out of reverse, and the submarine moved slowly, making a wide turn, until we were on the other side of the mysterious object.

"It looks the same on this side as it does on the other," I said.

"Yeah," Lyle agreed. "I was hoping that maybe we might be able to figure out what it was."

"Let's mark the coordinates and keep going," Shane said. "We don't have much more bottom time. We have to be careful not to use up all of our air."

Lyle adjusted a couple of dials and called out some numbers for Holly to write down.

"This way," Lyle explained, "if we want to come back to see this thing again, it will be easier to find. All we'll have to do is punch in the coordinates."

We left the strange object and kept going. There

wasn't much else to see except for a few more fish. None of which, however, were anywhere close to the size of the muskellunge we had seen. But we didn't care. Every moment that passed was exciting. It was the anticipation of what we *might* see that made the adventure so much fun.

We made it back to the boathouse just before dark. After mooring the *Independence* in the boathouse, we sat around and talked about our next underwater adventure. Puckett Lake was so big, we could spend the rest of the summer exploring! I just knew that we were in for some really cool adventures. We talked about borrowing a video camera so we could show our friends what we'd done. Shane said that he could probably borrow his dad's.

"Hey Parker!" Tony said to me. "You can even write a book about our adventures!"

"Maybe," I said. "It sure would make a cool story." I like to write a lot, and the more I thought about it, the more I liked the idea of writing about our adventures. Some people might like to read about the things we do.

And we pretty much forgot about the strange object that we'd seen. All of us . . . except Holly O'Mara. She'd been thinking about that thing ever since we came upon it at the bottom of the lake, and the very next morning she went to the Great Bear Heart Historical Museum to see if she could find out what it was.

Well, she found out what it was, all right. And when she told the rest of us what she thought it was, we all went bananas.

9

The following morning, we gathered at the boathouse to get ready for another day of exploring. Lyle and Shane got there long before we did. They wanted to go over the *Independence* from top to bottom to make sure she was in good shape. By ten o'clock, the day was getting warm . . . but there was no sign of Holly.

"Did she say she had to do something else today?" Shane asked the group.

Dylan shook his head. "I heard her say last night that she would be here," he said.

"That's strange," I said. It wasn't at all like Holly not to show up.

"Well, we can't sail without her," Lyle said, and just as he finished his sentence, we saw Holly coming toward us. She was crossing through the park, carrying a big book. Dollar was at her feet.

When she saw us, she broke into a jog. Dollar had to race to keep up with her. Holly stopped when she reached the dock.

"Sorry I'm late," she said excitedly, "but you're not going to believe what I found out!"

"About what?" Tony asked.

"You know that thing we found in deep water yesterday?" Holly asked.

"Yeah," we all said.

"Well, here's the story. A long time ago, there used to be a big hotel on the other side of the park. It was really popular and a lot of people stayed there.

"There was a time when it was illegal to gamble in Michigan. But at this hotel, there was a secret room in the basement where gangsters from different cities would come to gamble."

"But what does that have to do with what we found in the lake?" Dylan asked.

"I'm getting to that," Holly replied. "You see, it wasn't long before the police found out what was going on. They planned to raid the place one night, but somebody tipped off the gangsters."

"You mean somebody told them that the cops were on their way?" I asked.

Holly nodded. "That gave them time to get rid of all of their games and things. And they managed to take one of those things out into the lake and dump it overboard so the police wouldn't find it."

"What was it that they dumped in the lake?" Dylan asked. I thought his eyes were going to fall out of his head and plop into the water.

Holly opened up the book to an old black and white picture. "A slot machine," she said confidently. "That's what we found yesterday. The slot machine that the gangsters dumped overboard!"

She was right!

We all gathered around the book Holly was holding. There was a black and white picture of two men with dark suits and hats, sitting next to a slot machine. There was a pile of money on the table where they were sitting.

"That's it!" Lyle exclaimed. "That looks like it's the same size and shape of the thing we found yesterday!"

"And we all know what's inside slot machines," Holly said.

"Money!" we shouted in unison.

We could hardly believe our luck. Puckett Lake is pretty big. If we had set out purposely to find the slot machine, it would have been like looking for a needle in a haystack. We could have searched for years and never found it.

But we *had* found it . . . by accident. We found it without even knowing, at the time, what we'd found.

I looked at Shane. He had a wide grin on his face, and his eyes were on fire. "Do we even need to take a vote on this, guys?" he asked.

"No way!" we cheered.

And that's all it took. We might not ever find the silver dollars that the robbers had hidden all those years ago, but, by gosh, we knew where that slot machine was.

And the Adventure Club was going to go get it.

10

We had a lot of preparation to do, so we decided that we'd meet out at the new clubhouse later in the day to discuss ideas.

While we were certain we would be able to locate the slot machine again, we weren't so sure how we were going to get it to the surface.

"We can use the lift bags, just like we did with the submarine!" Dylan offered. "It'll just float right up to the surface!"

Shane shook his head. "If we were scuba divers, that might work," he said. "But remember: we had to swim down to the *Independence* to hook the bags to it. Then we had to swim down with the air hose. That slot machine is in a hundred and twenty feet of water. There's no way we can swim that deep."

"What if we made a robotic arm that we could control from inside the sub?" Tony suggested. "We could make a claw on it that could grab the slot machine."

"That would work," Lyle agreed, "but it would take us a long time to build it. Plus, it would cost money, and that's one thing that none of us has a lot of."

"What about just a simple hook?" Holly said. "One that could be welded to the outside of the sub? From the looks of the picture, the slot machine has a pull arm. The hook could be looped under the arm, and the sub could carry it back to the boathouse."

That seemed to be the best idea, and one that wouldn't cost any money. We could find the scrap metal at Franklin's junkyard, and Tony could borrow his dad's welding unit again.

Although we really wanted to take the sub out that day, we decided that we'd all work together to make the hook. The sooner we got the hook ready, the sooner we could retrieve the slot machine.

And man . . . we were excited! In my mind, I tried to

estimate how much money was in the slot machine. I didn't know much about them, but I know that some slot machines take quarters and some take dollars.

That would be so cool! A slot machine filled with dollars! It made us forget all about the silver dollars that were supposed to be hidden somewhere around Great Bear Heart.

The hook that we made was pretty simple. It was about as long as my arm, and the end curved up. We hoisted the sub up on the winch and Tony expertly welded it to the front of the sub, right beneath the viewing window. It didn't look pretty—like the *Independence* now had a weird hook-nose—but that was okay. It looked like it would get the job done, and that's all that mattered.

By the time we finished, however, it was late. All of us would have to be going home soon, so we wouldn't have the time to go and get the slot machine.

But first thing in the morning, we would. We would meet at the boathouse early, and then we would head out and retrieve the sunken slot machine.

We were going to be rich.

11

The next morning, I was up and out the door even before Mom and Dad were awake. I left them a note, grabbed a handful of cereal, and raced to the boathouse.

Holly was already there, seated on the dock, her legs dangling over the edge. Her shoes almost touched the water. Dollar sat next to her, staring down.

"Hi Holly," I said as I approached the dock.

"Hi Parker," she yawned. Dollar bounded to his feet and ran up to me.

"Hey there, little buddy," I said, kneeling and scratching the kitten behind his ears. Dollar rubbed up against my leg, arching his back, his tail weaving like a furry snake.

The sun was just beginning to rise on the other side of the lake. A couple of boats were on the water, and, not far from the dock, a few rings on the surface indicated where fish were feeding.

Soon, Dylan came riding up on his bicycle, followed by Shane, Tony, and Lyle. Shane's hair was sticking up in all sorts of different directions, and it was obvious that he'd just gotten out of bed. He looked pretty funny.

Holly scooped up Dollar, and we piled into the sub without saying much. I don't know if it was because we were so excited, or because we were all tired.

"Main hatch closed," Shane said as he twisted the airlock wheel.

"Excellent work, Captain Mitchell," Lyle said. "Crew . . . prepare for departure."

Which was kind of funny, since there really wasn't a lot for any of us to do.

Lights blinked on, and the engine roared to life.

"Coordinates, Captain O'Mara," Lyle said. Holly placed Dollar on the floor, reached into her pocket, and pulled out her notepad. She read off some numbers, and Lyle typed them into a small keypad on the control panel.

"It should take us about ten minutes," Lyle said as

the *Independence* pulled away from the dock.

"We're going to have to be careful on the way back," Holly warned, pointing to the long hook that extended out from below the viewing window. "After we hook that slot machine, we won't be able to go very fast, otherwise it might fall off."

"Holly's right," Shane said. "We'll have to go slow."

True to Lyle's word, we reached the slot machine in about ten minutes. Tony Gritter was once again in charge of the spotlight, and the goo-covered object suddenly appeared in the bright beam.

"There it is!" Dylan exclaimed, pointing.

Lyle slowed the submarine, and we approached the object slowly. We all leaned forward, peering over Lyle's shoulder to see the looming object.

"Try and put the hook right under that arm," Holly said. "Then rise up just a little bit and see what happens."

Lyle carefully guided the sub up to the machine. Hooking the arm of the slot machine was even harder than it looked. Twice when Lyle had placed the hook under the arm, the machine slipped off. Once, it nearly fell over. Layers of silt drifted off like smoke in the still water, and globs of goo and zebra mussels fell off and dropped to the bottom.

"Arrgh," Lyle groaned.

"No, you've got it, you've got it," Holly assured him. "Just go slower this time."

And it worked. We held our breath as Lyle guided the hook under the arm of the slot machine. Then he guided the sub upward, and the slot machine came with it.

"You got it!" Tony exclaimed, slapping Lyle on the shoulder.

"We're not home yet," Lyle said. "We have a long way to go."

Slowly, Lyle turned the submarine around, and we started back at a snail's pace. We went extra slow on our return trip, knowing that if we weren't careful, the slot machine would slip off. It took us nearly half an hour to make it back to the boathouse.

"How are we going to get the thing on shore?" Dylan asked.

"I think the best way," Lyle said, "is to drop it near the dock. Then we can moor the sub, and we can get into the water and carry it to shore. It's pretty heavy, and it's going to take all of us to move it."

"That's because it's filled with money!" Tony

exclaimed. "I can't wait to see all of those coins!"

By turning the submarine sideways a little, the slot machine became unbalanced and slipped off, falling to the sand in an explosion of silty debris.

"Bingo!" Shane said, and Lyle spun the sub around and headed for the boathouse. In minutes we'd moored the *Independence*, and were ready to retrieve the slot machine.

And I'll say this: Lyle was right. That thing was *heavy*. It took all six of us just to drag it to shallow water. Then we had to pick it up and carry it to the shore, which was nearly impossible. We had to carry it a few feet, rest, carry it a little farther, rest again. It took us another half hour just to get it close to the boathouse.

But we did it. As the sun bore down on us, we stood on the shore, panting, water dripping off of our chins and noses. The slot machine sat upright in the grass, all caked with years of mud, goop, and goo. Tony scraped the zebra mussels off with his pocket knife. Now that it was out of the water, we could make out a few more features. It was definitely a slot machine, that's for sure.

"Let's open it!" Dylan exclaimed.

"Not so fast," I said. "Let's clean it up. Right now, it's so dirty that there's no way of knowing where it opens."

"And another thing we didn't think about," Shane said. "It's probably locked, like a safe. We might have to break into it."

"Let's lift it into the boathouse," Holly said. "We can lock it inside while we go and get some cleaning stuff."

That seemed like a good idea, so we hefted the bulky machine into the boathouse. Lyle locked the door, and we walked up to the Great Bear Heart Market.

"All right, who's got money?" Shane asked.

We all looked at each other.

"I don't have any money," I said. "I'm in my bathing suit. And I only have couple dollars at home."

"I don't have any money on me, either," Dylan piped. "And I don't have *any* money at home."

"Same here," Tony said. "I'm so broke, I can't even pay attention."

Which was pretty funny, when you think about it.

"All right," Shane said, "here's what we do. Each of us needs to go home and get as much cleaning stuff as we can find. Brushes, soap . . . stuff like that. Let's meet back at the boathouse in twenty minutes."

I liked that idea better. I didn't want to spend my money on cleaning supplies. Neither did anyone else, I imagine.

Twenty minutes. In twenty minutes, we'd be meeting at the boathouse, where we would clean up the slot machine and open it up. Oh, I knew that there was a good chance that it was locked, but I also knew we'd figure out a way to get inside.

I *knew* it.

What I didn't know was that while we were gone, someone had gotten past the locked doors of the boathouse.

And they were still inside, waiting for us when we came back.

12

I stuffed a bunch of cleaning supplies—detergents, some spray cleaner I found under the sink, and some paper towels—into my backpack so I could ride my bike back to the boathouse without having to carry an armload of stuff. Lyle Haywood had just got there, and he was hopping off his bike. He, too, had a backpack filled with cleaning supplies.

"I think we'll have enough stuff to clean the whole town," I said.

He laughed as he pulled the key to the boathouse from his pocket. "I think you're right," he chuckled.

Dylan rode up, huffing and puffing. He was carrying

a bottle of spray cleaner and a box of steel wool in one arm. He hopped off his bike and propped it against the boathouse.

Lyle fumbled with the lock, then pulled the large door open. He stopped. His eyes grew wide as he stared into the boathouse.

"Surprise!" I heard three voices chime from inside the boathouse . . . and instantly, I knew who the voices belonged to.

The Martin brothers.

"How . . . when . . . ?" Lyle stammered as he opened the door wider, and then I could see them. The three brothers were sitting on the dock next to the submarine, their feet dangling in the water. They wore only their bathing suits, and they were sopping wet.

And I suddenly realized how they'd gotten inside.

The boathouse is made for boats. It's like an actual garage built so that a boat can float inside of it. Around the inside perimeter is a dock walkway about three feet wide. There is a big door on the front, but it only goes down to the waterline. Normally, people wouldn't be able to get inside, because there is a padlock on the door.

What the Martins must have done, however, was swam *under* the door. The submarine inside didn't take up as much space as a boat, so they wouldn't have any problem swimming in and climbing up onto the dock.

"Hey!" Dylan said when he saw the three boys inside. "You can't be here!"

Gary looked at Terry. "I'm here," he said arrogantly. "You here, Terry?"

"I sure am, Gary. How 'bout you, Larry?"

"As here as here can be," Larry smirked.

Gary looked at Dylan and frowned. "Looks like we're here."

Shane Mitchell arrived, and right behind him was Holly O'Mara. When they saw the three brothers in the boathouse, they gasped.

"What are you doing here?!?!" Shane demanded.

"Just seeing what *you* were doing here," Larry replied. "You guys have been awfully sneaky about what you're doing."

"And now we know why," Gary said, nodding at the *Independence.*

"What we do here is none of your business!" Holly said.

"Hey . . . we were just being neighborly, and paying you guys a visit. We think the least you could do is take us for a ride in your sub."

"Fat chance," Shane spat. "We're not taking you for a ride anywhere."

"Especially not after what you did to our clubhouse!" Dylan fumed.

The three Martins feigned surprise. "Why, I don't know what you're talking about," Terry said. "Do you, Gary?"

Gary shook his head. "Not a clue," he said.

"Get out of here, you guys," Lyle demanded. "This place doesn't belong to you."

"Well, why don't you just make us leave, you skinny twerp," Gary sneered.

"Yeah," Larry chimed. "What are *you* going to do about it?"

We were in a bad spot. None of us wanted to get into a fight, even though there was five of us and three of them. The Martins are older than we are, and they're bigger, too.

I heard footsteps approaching, and Tony appeared around the side of the boathouse. And right behind him . . . .

Mr. Bloomer, the owner of the Great Bear Heart Market!

Tony had a big smile on his face. When Gary Martin saw him, he was about to say something . . . but when he saw Mr. Bloomer right behind him, he didn't say a word. All three boys knew they'd been caught.

"I think it's time for you guys to go home," Mr. Bloomer said, hiking his thumb in the air. "Now."

Grudgingly, the three Martins stood up. They walked past us without a word.

"And don't forget," Mr. Bloomer continued as the Martins walked away. "I know your father real well. If you guys start causing trouble, don't think that I won't make a phone call or pay a visit."

We watched as the Martin brothers walked away. We could see them whispering to one another as they crossed the road. When they disappeared, I turned to Mr. Bloomer.

"Gosh, thanks Mr. Bloomer!" I said.

"You sure told them!" Dylan echoed.

"Yeah, thanks," Holly said.

"No problem," Mr. Bloomer said. "Let me know if they give you any more trouble. I really *do* know their father, and he won't be happy if he finds out that his kids are causing problems in town."

After Mr. Bloomer had gone, Tony explained.

"When I got near the boathouse, I heard the voices of the Martins. I looked through a crack in the back of the boathouse and saw them sitting on the edge of the dock, so I ran back to the market and told Mr. Bloomer what was happening. He doesn't like the Martin brothers, anyway, so he was happy to come down and kick them out."

"Good thinking!" Shane said.

"I'm sure we haven't seen the last of them," I said.

"Parker's right," Lyle said with a nod. "From now on, we're going to have to keep an eye out for them and be really careful."

"I'm glad they didn't do anything to the slot machine," Holly said, pointing to the mud-caked object in the boathouse.

"Yeah," Shane said. "Come on. Let's get it cleaned up."

We got to work. It took hours of scraping and scrubbing. The slot machine had been in the water for so long that the mud seemed like it had become a part of the metal. Even after we'd finished, a lot of the metal remained tarnished.

And Shane was right. There was a keyhole on the back of the unit that, quite obviously, required a key to open a square, metal door. We wondered how we were going to get the thing unlocked.

Tony shook his head. "Guys," he said, picking up a screwdriver. "That thing has been at the bottom of the lake for seventy years or more. That lock will break easy."

Without another word he inserted the blade of the screwdriver into the lock. He tapped it a little to force it in. Then he gave it a hard turn.

There was a loud *snap!* and a springing sound, and the lock turned. While we gathered close, Tony removed the screwdriver and pried open the square door.

13

The compartment was empty.

We all groaned. There wasn't any money inside the slot machine, after all. The only thing the compartment contained was water and slime.

"Well, we should have known," Holly said with a shrug. "If there really *had* been any money inside, we would have heard it jingling around."

"Hey, it's still pretty cool," Shane said.

"But what are we going to do with it?" Dylan asked. "Sell it?"

"It's probably worth some money," Lyle said. "Why don't we take it down to the historical museum? They might know how much it's worth."

"Good idea," Shane said. "But it will break our backs if we have to carry it all the way down there."

"I'll run home and get my wagon!" Dylan said. "We can put it in my wagon and wheel 'er on down to the museum!"

Dylan returned a few minutes later pulling a red wagon. We lifted the slot machine up and carefully set it inside. Tony pulled the wagon, and the rest of us walked alongside to keep it from falling over, in case we hit a bump.

Fortunately, the Great Bear Heart Historical Museum wasn't far away. It's located in the same building as the Great Bear Heart Public Library. The building itself is the old railroad depot, and behind it is the park with a small beach. The railroad tracks were torn up long ago, but the old railroad bed is now a trail for hiking, skiing, and biking.

We wheeled the whole wagon inside the museum, and when the lady at the desk saw what we had, she about fell out of her chair.

"Where did you . . . how . . . when . . . ?" she stammered. She was so excited she couldn't even finish her sentence.

"We found it in the lake," Holly said proudly. "I think it's the same one that I saw in the book you let me borrow."

"It is, it is!" the woman shrieked, stepping around the desk. She walked up to the slot machine and stared at it. "How on earth did you find it?!?!"

"Oh, we have a submarine," Shane said. "We were exploring the lake and we found it. We were wondering if it was worth any money."

"Well, I'm sure it's worth something," the woman replied. "But I'll tell you what. This would make a very nice addition to our museum. We have a small budget to buy things that are of historical value to the community. I would like to buy it, if you would sell it to the museum."

"For how much?" I asked.

"Oh, I'm afraid I couldn't pay you more than a hundred dollars," she replied, still marveling at the old slot machine.

"A HUNDRED DOLLARS!?!?!" we all shouted at the same time.

"I'm afraid that's all we can afford," she replied. "The museum doesn't have a lot of money."

"We'll take it!" Shane exclaimed.

"You bet!" Tony replied.

The lady walked back around to her desk, retrieved a pair of keys, and unlocked a drawer. She opened it up and pulled out five crisp, twenty-dollar bills.

"There you go," she said, holding out the money.

We were so shocked that we couldn't move. We just stared at the money in her hand. Finally, Lyle Haywood stepped up.

"Thank you," he said, taking the money.

"Yeah, thanks," I said. "Thanks a ton!"

We lifted the slot machine from the wagon and placed it in a corner.

"That'll be fine, right there," she said. "At least for now. Thank you again."

When we left, it felt like we were walking in the clouds.

Later that day, we met at our new clubhouse to discuss what we would do with the money. We used to keep our cash in a coffee can hidden in the woods, but with the snoopy Martin brothers around we decided that it wasn't a good idea anymore. Holly O'Mara is our club treasurer, so it was decided that she would hold onto the money until we needed it for something.

A hundred dollars, I thought as I climbed the rope

ladder up to our clubhouse. *That's a lot of money.*

I climbed through the trap door. Lyle Haywood was already there, along with Tony Gritter.

"Hey guys," I said.

"We've got it!" Tony exclaimed.

"You've got what?" I asked, taking a seat on a milk crate.

"Lyle and I figured out what we're going to do with the money," Tony answered.

My eyes lit up. "Yeah? What?"

"Wait until everybody shows up," Lyle said. "But it's something that would be really cool."

After everyone arrived, Lyle and Tony explained their idea.

"We've all wanted to go to Mackinac Island," Tony explained. Which was true. Mackinac Island is in Lake Huron. It's about thirty miles from Great Bear Heart. There are lots of houses and shops on the island, along with an old fort that's a few hundred years old. The island is a really popular place. To get there, you have to take a ferry boat. And there are no cars allowed on the island, so you either have to walk, bike, or ride in a horse carriage to get around. There are lots of things to see and do on the island. There's even a gigantic building called

Grand Hotel that is one of the biggest hotels in the world. It was built way back in 1887. There are even a few ghost stories about the place. We'd all wanted to see what it looked like up close.

"What do you think?" Lyle said. "We could use the money to pay for our ferry tickets to the island. Plus, we'd still have money left over. We could split it up among ourselves and be able to buy souvenirs if we wanted."

Dylan leapt from his milk crate. "That would be totally super-cool!"

"Yeah," I agreed. "I've been to Mackinac Island, but I didn't get to do much exploring."

"How would we get to the ferry?" Holly asked.

Good question. We would have to take a ferry from Mackinaw City, which was about a half-hour drive from Great Bear Heart.

"Easy," Lyle said. "My mom works in Mackinaw City. We could catch a ride with her in the morning. She could drop us off, and we could take the nine o'clock ferry to the island. Then we could take the four-thirty ferry back to Mackinaw City, and arrive at about the time that Mom is getting off work, so she could drive us back home."

"We'd have the whole day on the island!" Tony said.

And that was that. We took a quick vote and decided that we'd start planning our trip to Mackinac Island. We were all excited about spending the day there. What an adventure that would be!

But it would be much more than that. For sure, it would be a lot of fun, and we would all have a good time.

However, something was going to happen at the Grand Hotel that, to this day, creeps me out when I think about it. And you may have even heard the rumors about Grand Hotel being haunted. There are lots of stories about ghosts in the hotel.

Well, they aren't just *stories.* They're true. *All* of them.

And the six of us in the Adventure Club were about to find out.

GHOST IN THE GRAND

1

As luck would have it, we were able to visit Mackinac Island that very same week. Friday would be the day.

We all had things to do before we left for our trip. Holly was in charge of making sandwiches. Dylan wanted to be in charge of food, but we remembered how awful his sandwiches had tasted from the last time. What we decided was that Holly would make the sandwiches, and Dylan could help. We all pitched in by 'donating' some of the food that each of us scrounged up from our own houses. I snagged a full loaf of bread and some strawberry jam, Tony sneaked a whole jar of peanut butter, and so on. Holly was able to make two sandwiches for each of us, which would save us money on the island. We dipped into the cash just a little bit to buy twelve cans of lemonade—two for each of us—so we wouldn't get too thirsty.

Originally, we wanted to bring our bikes with us, but Lyle's mom said no. She said there was no way she was going to be able to fit six kids and six bikes in her van. And she wasn't strapping any on the roof, either, which is what Shane suggested. We could rent bikes on the island, but, again, we wouldn't have a lot of money left over after we paid for the ferry tickets, and we wanted to save what we could.

Lyle's mom dropped us off at the ferry dock just before nine. Each of us carried our own backpack with our sandwiches and lemonades. I carried a first aid kit (you never know when one of those things can come in handy) and a book. I knew I probably wouldn't read it at all, but I've always been that way. Anytime I go on a trip somewhere, I always take a book with me. The one I was reading was about werewolves in Wisconsin.

"Be back by five o'clock," Lyle's mom said to us as we scrambled out of the van.

"Sure thing, Mrs. Haywood," Tony said.

"And you guys be careful," she said.

"Don't worry, Mom," Lyle said. "We'll be fine."

Mrs. Haywood gave one last wave and drove off.

"This is going to be so cool!" Dylan said, slinging his backpack over his shoulder.

"Awesome!" Holly exclaimed.

"*Totally* awesome!" I added.

And we were right. It was going to be cool, awesome and exciting.

But it would also be something else.

It would be terrifying.

2

Holly waited in line at the ticket counter. There were a ton of people all over the place! People come from all over the world to Mackinac Island. It's one of the most popular places to visit in Michigan.

And we were going to be there for the whole day!

We boarded the big ferry boat at nine. The boats that are used to transport people back and forth are huge! The one we boarded had an upper and a lower deck. We climbed to the upper deck, which was completely open.

"That's where we're going, guys," I said, pointing to Mackinac Island in the distance. Holly had brought a disposable camera, and she clicked off a few shots.

BREGE '03

"And look!" Dylan exclaimed. "You can even see the Grand Hotel from here!"

Dylan was right. Grand Hotel was enormous, and we could see its long, white shape nestled on the southern bluff of Mackinac Island. It seemed to glow in the morning sun.

"I want to see the fort," said Holly.

"Me too," said Lyle. "Just think . . . there were actually battles fought on the island!"

"I'm going to buy some fudge!" said Tony. That's one of the things that Mackinac Island is famous for: fudge. You can smell it when you walk down Main Street.

The ride across the Straits of Mackinac took us about twenty minutes. To the west, we saw the gigantic span of the Mackinac Bridge that connects Michigan's upper and lower peninsulas. The bridge is five miles long! Cars and trucks crossing the bridge looked like tiny ants from where we were on the ferry.

And we'd lucked out with the weather, too. The temperature was seventy-five degrees, and there wasn't a cloud in the sky. A perfect day to visit Mackinac Island.

Twenty minutes later, we arrived at the island. Everywhere we looked, people milled about. Horse drawn carriages were everywhere, taking people on tours or to one of the island hotels. A big black carriage with two big black horses waited near a curb.

"Check that out!" I exclaimed, pointing. "That looks like something out of an old movie!"

"Okay," Shane said. "We all have things that we want to do. Why don't we pair up, and at noon we'll all meet up at Grand Hotel?"

"Fine with me," Holly said. "Lyle . . . you wanna go to the fort?"

"Yeah," Lyle said.

"Tony and I'll go check out Mission Point Resort," Shane said, and Tony nodded. Mission Point Resort is another big hotel on the island.

"Where do you want to go?" I asked Dylan.

"I don't care," he replied shaking his head. "I'm just glad to be here!"

"Cool," I said. "Then we'll explore downtown and maybe some of the areas around the town. Then we'll meet you guys up at the Grand."

We went our separate ways. And I will say this: Dylan was more excited that day than I had ever seen him. I was excited, too, but I thought Dylan was going to jump out of his skin. He was *that* excited.

We hiked up and down Main Street and went into a few shops. Then we walked up to the fort, which sits high on a hill. From there, you can see for miles and miles. You can see Michigan's lower peninsulas, and Bois Blanc island to the east. And we could also see the Round Island lighthouse, which used to help to guide ships to the island.

But we didn't see Holly or Lyle. The fort is a pretty big place, and we figured that they were busy exploring some other part.

At noon, we hiked up to the Grand Hotel. All around us were people walking and horse drawn carriages. We could hear the clip-clop, clip-clop of hooves on pavement long before the horses passed by.

"Wow!" Dylan exclaimed as the Grand Hotel came into view. "That thing is huge!"

"Bigger than huge," I said. "It looks like a skyscraper on its side!"

When we arrived at the front of the hotel, Lyle, Holly, Dylan and Shane were already there.

"We're not late, are we?" I asked as I looked at my watch. It was a few minutes before twelve.

Tony shook his head. "You're right on time. We got here early, that's all."

People were everywhere. Not only is Grand Hotel a gigantic old structure, but it also has the world's largest porch—over 880 feet long! There were dozens of people clustered in groups on the porch, sitting in chairs, talking and laughing. Some people were just standing or sitting quietly, alone, enjoying the view and the pleasant weather. Still more people were in the huge yard in front of the hotel.

Holly pulled out her camera and backed away from us. "Everybody smile!" she said, and clicked off a picture. Then she returned her camera to her backpack and rejoined the group.

"It sure would be cool to walk around and explore some of the rooms," Lyle said.

"I don't know if we'd be allowed to," Shane said.

"I'd like to go around back and see some of the horses," Holly said, which sounded like a good idea. We walked around the building and to the stable, completely unaware of what was about to happen.

3

One of the ghost stories about the Grand Hotel goes like this:

About a hundred years ago, the hotel was filled with guests. People were eating and talking, sipping tea and relaxing. It was just another day at the hotel. Well, as the story goes, dozens of people claimed to see strange things happen. Objects that moved by themselves, things like that. Everyone fled the hotel in a panic, and it took a while before anyone wanted to stay at the Grand Hotel again.

Of course, that's just a story. There are other ghost stories about the place, but I've never really believed them.

At the stable behind the hotel, carriages were coming and going. Not far off was a livery stable.

"I'll bet that's where they keep the horses," Holly said. "Want to go check it out?"

"Yeah, let's go," Dylan said, and the six of us walked over to the stable.

Horses were everywhere. Big ones, black ones, brown ones, all different kinds. Some stood in stalls, others were being led around the barn by their handlers.

Nearby, an old man stood next to a huge, black horse. He held one of the horse's hooves in his hand. When he looked up, he saw us staring at him. His hair was white as snow, and he had a thick mustache that was just as white. His face was wrinkled with age, and his blue eyes glowed. When he saw us, he smiled.

"Hello, young friends, hello," he said. His voice was deep and gravelly. He let go of the horse's hoof and stood up straight. "And what can I help you with?"

"Oh, we were just kind of checking the place out," Shane said.

"Well, there are certainly a lot of things to see here," the old man said with a smile. "As you can see, the livery stable is a busy place."

He told us that he was a farrier, and he helped take care of the horses. He was even nice enough to show us around. We got to see some of the horses up close, and even pet a couple of them.

"Thanks for the tour," Lyle said when we were finished. "I hope we didn't take you away from anything."

"Not at all," the old man said.

"Wait!" Holly said, slipping off her backpack. She pulled out her disposable camera. "Can we take a picture?"

"Sure," the man said.

We asked one of the other workers to take a picture, and the six of us posed with the old man and one of the horses. The man took a picture using Holly's camera.

"Thanks," we all said.

"Not a problem," the old man replied. "Are you going to look around inside the Grand?"

"We'd like to," I said, "but we're not guests."

"Oh, you can go in and look around. There is a service door in the back that is rarely used. Just don't get into trouble."

"A secret door?" Dylan gasped.

The old man laughed. "Not a 'secret' door," he

explained. "A 'service' door. It's a door for the hotel workers. I'll show you where it is. You kids go inside and look around all you want. If anyone gives you any trouble, you just tell them that you're my guests."

"What about ghosts?" Dylan asked.

"Ghosts?" the old man replied with a frown. Then he nodded. "Ah, you've heard the stories. Well, all I can say is this: I've worked here my whole life, and I've never seen a ghost. There are lots of stories, but I don't think any of them are true."

He led us out of the livery stable and to a door at the back of the hotel.

"You can go in here," he said. "This will take you to the main hallway. Just remember . . . when you want to leave, you must leave through these doors."

"How come?" Dylan asked.

"It's because . . . well—" The old man paused and gazed up thoughtfully. "They won't let you leave out of the other doors. You'll have to come back through this door."

He opened the door, and we walked through.

"Have fun," he said, and the door closed behind us. We were alone in a long, narrow, empty hall.

"Cool!" Tony said, his voice echoing. "We get to see

the inside of the Grand Hotel!"

We walked along the thin corridor until we reached a wide hallway—and we noticed right away that something wasn't quite right.

I stopped and stared. Tony noticed it, too, and he stopped and gasped.

Holly, Shane, Lyle and Dylan stopped dead in their tracks. We all stared. We couldn't believe what we were seeing.

4

"Are they having some sort of party?" I asked.

"It's the Grand Hotel," Shane said. "They're probably always having some sort of party."

There were dozens of people all around, but they were all dressed in old clothing . . . clothing that people would have worn years and years ago.

"It's like everyone is in costume," Dylan said. "Geez . . . they sure look funny."

"What's going on?" Tony asked as he gazed around.

"I don't know," Holly replied. "But every single person seems to be dressed in old clothes."

"It's like we traveled back in time or something,"

Lyle said. "Like that movie that they filmed here where the guy goes back in time." Years ago, there was a movie made at the Grand Hotel about a man who traveled back in time. That's kind of how we felt, looking at the way everyone was dressed.

"We're the only people wearing normal clothes," Tony said.

"Or the only oddballs," Shane said.

"Come on," I urged. "Let's go check out the place."

We strode down the hall and through the main lobby. Suddenly, we found ourselves in a very large room. There were people everywhere, and they were all dressed in old clothing. It was actually kind of creepy.

"Parker," Holly whispered to me, *"there's no way that all these people had time to go and change their clothing. We were outside twenty minutes ago, watching people go in and out, and everyone was dressed normally. Now, not a single person is dressed in the modern clothing of today."*

Now that Holly mentioned it, it really *was* weird. It was like some gigantic costume party where everyone dressed up in clothing from a hundred years ago.

All except us. We were all wearing modern clothing, and I felt really out of place.

A man was standing at a desk not far away. He was

smiling and watching people. Holly pulled out her camera and took a picture of him.

"Let's go ask *him,*" Shane said, and we walked up to the desk.

"Excuse me," Shane said, "but is this some sort of costume party?"

The man didn't say anything. In fact, he acted like he didn't hear Shane at all.

"Pardon me?" Shane said a little louder, trying to get the man's attention.

Still, the man just stared around the room, smiling and nodding at other people.

Shane reached out and waved his hands in front of the man's face, snapping his fingers.

"Hello?" he said. "Can you hear me? Can you see me?"

"Man, that dude's rude," Dylan said quietly.

Just then, a waiter passed by. "Excuse me," I said, but I never got a chance to finish. The waiter walked by us like we weren't even there.

"Maybe we're not supposed to be here," I said. "That's why everyone is ignoring us."

"If we weren't supposed to be here, somebody would have told us by now," Tony said.

We just stood there, off to the side, watching people milling about, talking, and laughing. No one seemed to notice us.

"Wait a minute," Holly said. She took a step toward a group of three ladies. The women were talking to each other. Holly walked right up and stood right in the middle of the three women.

"What's she doing?" Dylan whispered.

Holly started waving her arms in front of the women! Then she started jumping up and down and yelling loudly, but the women didn't pay any attention to her! They acted like she wasn't even there!

Finally, Holly walked back to us.

"It's like they're ghosts or something," she said. Her voice was trembling. I could tell she was frightened. "I was standing right in front of them, and it was like they were looking right through me."

Could that be it? I thought. *Could all of these people around us be . . . ghosts?*

I shivered. Just the thought of being surrounded by so many ghosts gave me the chills.

"Come on," Shane said. "We've got to find out what's going on. Let's go to the front desk."

We wandered through the great hall. Still, no one

paid any attention to us. Nobody looked at us, nobody smiled at us. It was bizarre.

We walked up to the front desk. Two men and a woman were standing behind it.

Once again, the same thing happened. Shane tried to talk to them, and he was ignored. But when another man and a woman walked up to the desk, they smiled and talked and were very helpful.

I turned to Holly and was about to say something, but the expression on her face caused me to pause. She was staring at the desk. Her eyes were wide, and her face was white. She looked terrified.

It was a book. Holly was looking at a large book on the desk. While we watched, the man and woman in front of us signed their names. When they walked away, we stepped up closer.

The book was open. At the top of both pages were the words 'Guest Registry - Grand Hotel, Mackinac Island.' Beneath the headings were ink scrawlings where guests had signed their names.

And suddenly, we all realized what Holly had been so freaked out about.

The date on the registry read July 24th, 1908.

5

"This is impossible!" Lyle said. "There is no such thing as time travel!"

"It's got to be some kind of joke," I said.

Tony shook his head. "Well, it makes sense," he said. "Maybe that's why these people can't see us. If it's 1908, we haven't even been born yet!"

"Heck, my dad hasn't been born yet," Shane added.

"That would mean that these people aren't ghosts," Holly said quietly. She paused, and we looked at her. "*We* are," she said. "*We're* the ghosts."

Holly's words freaked us out. To think that we had somehow become ghosts was unimaginable.

Another waiter walked by, and Lyle reached out and grabbed his arm. "Hey," he began, but he didn't finish. The waiter suddenly dropped the empty silver tray he was carrying. It made an awful crashing sound as it hit the floor, and a lot of people looked at him. The waiter looked around, almost directly at Lyle, but he didn't see him. Confused, he scratched his head for a moment and continued to look around. Then he picked up the tray and hustled off.

"Oh my gosh!" Lyle said. "I caused him to drop the tray!"

"Man, we're going to have to be really careful," Tony said.

"Careful?" Holly said. "I don't want to be careful! I want to go back to where we belong! Back to our time!"

"Yeah, me too," Dylan said. "This is too weird."

"But guys . . . think about it!" Shane said. "How many people do you know that have actually been able to go back in time and see what it's really like? I mean . . . we can read books or watch movies, but we're really *here!*" He looked around. "I'll bet nobody else has ever had this kind of experience!"

"Shane is right," I said. "It might be cool to hang

out and look around."

"Yeah," said Tony. "Just think: when we go back to school and we have to write an essay about what we did on our summer vacation, this will be great!"

Holly seemed to calm down a little. "I guess it would be okay to look around for a little while," she said. "But not for too long."

"All in favor of hanging out in 1908 for a while raise their hands," Shane said.

It was unanimous. We would stay for a while and see what things were like at the Grand Hotel in the year 1908. I had no idea how it happened, or even why it happened, but we were here. We were here, and it was real.

However, there was one important fact that we overlooked . . . and we all realized what it was when Tony Gritter walked over to one of the doors to the porch, grasped the knob, and pulled.

6

The swung open, startling several guests standing nearby.

"Did you see that?" a woman gasped. "The door opened all by itself!

"Remarkable," someone said.

All of a sudden, we realized that although they couldn't see us, they could see the door opening! To the people watching, it looked like the door opened on its own!

A man cautiously walked over to the door, and Tony had to leap out of his way. The man closed the door and looked at it curiously. "I don't know how that happened," the man said.

"Perhaps it was a ghost," another man said with a chuckle. "I've heard that there are ghosts that haunt the Grand Hotel."

Tony's eyes widened, and a mischievous grin spread across his face. He looked over at us, then he faced the man by the door. When the man walked away to join his group of friends, Tony reached out and opened the door again.

The crowd of people standing near the door gasped as it swung open. Tony giggled, and stepped back. This time, two men came and inspected the door.

"Must be the wind," one of the men said.

The other man stepped through the door, then stepped back in. "There's hardly a breeze at all," he said. "Strange. Very strange."

He closed the door, and the two men stood in front of it, like they were waiting for it to open again. I thought for a moment that Tony was going to open the door again, but he didn't. He stayed clear of the crowd and walked back to us.

"That was funny," he said. "They thought a ghost was doing it!"

"Well, that's what you are, sort of," Lyle said. "We can see them, but they can't see us."

"That's cool!" Dylan said. "We can go around and haunt the hotel! We can make everybody think that the place is haunted!"

"That would be fun!" I said. "There are lots of things that we could do to make people think that the Grand Hotel is haunted!"

"I don't know," Holly said. "That might scare people off."

"Oh, we won't scare them too bad," Tony said. Lyle and Shane were smiling, and I could tell that they thought it might be kind of fun. "Watch."

Tony walked over to where a man was serving tea to a group of people. He picked up an empty teacup from the tray.

Instantly, a horrified gasp washed over the crowd. People drew back, their mouths open in shock, eyes wide with fear. We knew that what they were seeing wasn't a kid holding a teacup. All they were seeing was a cup suspended in the air all by itself!

"Oh my!" a lady shrieked.

"That's . . . that's impossible!" a man exclaimed.

"That's funny!" Lyle said, and he darted over to Tony and picked up the whole tray.

The crowd gasped again. By now, most of the

people in the great hall were transfixed, watching in terrified amazement as a teacup and a silver tray dangled in the air all by themselves. Of course, that's not what it looked like to us. We could see Tony and Lyle as clear as anything.

What happened next was sheer pandemonium. A voice from the crowd suddenly shrieked: "You see! Grand Hotel *is* haunted! There's the proof, right there! There is a ghost in the Grand!"

People began to flee, some of them running. They bumped into each other, dropping plates and cups and trays. Someone even knocked over a chair.

Tony set down the cup, and Lyle placed the tray on a table.

"Hey," Tony said. "Where's everybody going?"

"You scared them away," Holly said scornfully. "You shouldn't have done that."

Soon, there wasn't a single person anywhere. There was no one in the great room, no one in the halls, not a single person at the front desk. Everybody, it seemed, had been scared off by the pranks of Tony and Lyle.

Then I suddenly realized something.

"Guys!" I exclaimed. "Do you know what this means?!?!"

"Yeah," Tony smirked. "It means that everyone in 1908 was a fraidy-cat."

"Not hardly," I said. "It means that there is no ghost in the Grand! The stories of it being haunted aren't true!"

Holly suddenly realized what I was getting at. "Parker's right!" she said. "*We* were the ghosts they were talking about in those stories! Somehow, we've traveled back in time. The stories that we heard about ghosts in the Grand had nothing to do with ghosts!"

"Oh, I get it!" Dylan said. "Those stories were made up because of what Tony and Lyle did!"

"Hah!" Tony exclaimed, slapping Lyle's hand in a high-five. "We're famous! We're the ghosts in the Grand!"

Well, we were right . . . but we were also *wrong*.

Just because we thought that we were the 'ghosts' in the Grand Hotel didn't mean we were the *only* ghosts . . . and we were about to find out just how horrifying a *real* haunted hotel can be.

7

What happened next was really odd.

We were alone in the hotel . . . and I mean *completely* alone. It seemed that everyone—guests and workers—had been frightened off. Only a few minutes ago, there were dozens, if not *hundreds* of people milling about.

Now there was no one.

The Grand Hotel was empty.

"This is kind of spooky," Dylan said as we looked around. His voice echoed around the large, empty room. "Where did everybody go?"

I walked over to the window and looked outside.

From where I stood, I could see the Michigan mainland off in the distance. The Grand Hotel sits on a bluff, and below is a beautiful, landscaped yard with bright green grass, well-groomed trees, and colorful flowers. A path wound through the lush, green lawn.

But there weren't any people anywhere.

"There's nobody outside," I said.

"No one is on the porch, either," said Shane.

"Something funny is going on here," Holly said warily. "I mean . . . we scared everybody off, but they disappeared too quickly."

"Like they just vanished," Lyle mused.

"Let's search the hotel," I suggested. "There are three more floors, I think. Maybe we'll find some people on other floors."

"Let's stick together," Shane said. Normally, if we were going to search for something, we'd split up, but we all thought it would be best if, at least this time, we stayed in one group.

We didn't really know our way around, but Lyle noticed a staircase leading up. "Let's go up there," he said. "I'll bet that will take us to the next floor."

As we walked up the polished wood steps, I turned around. There was a banquet room with hundreds of tables . . . all of them empty of people. Half-eaten plates of food and glasses of water sat on expensive-looking tablecloths. It was like everyone just got up and walked away, right in the middle of their meal.

The stairs led up to the second floor. The hall was tall and wide. Closed doors lined each wall, and there were a few chairs and tables in the hall for guests to rest. Lyle tried opening one of the doors, but it was locked.

"There's nobody here, either," Holly whispered.

"Do you think we should go?" Dylan asked in a hushed voice.

"No, not yet," Shane replied thoughtfully. "Let's try and find out what's going on here."

We walked quietly to the end of the long hall. It ended at a pair of dark double doors.

"End of the road," Tony said. "Looks like we go back."

I tried the double doors, but they were locked, too, just like the others.

We turned around to walk back to the stairs, and suddenly, all six of us were gripped by a venomous fear.

At the other end of the hall, right in front of the stairs, was a horse and rider. They were staring at us, watching us, I was certain.

The hall was plenty big enough for a horse and rider, that was for sure. I didn't know how a horse and rider would actually get to the second floor . . . but that wasn't the horrifying part.

The horrifying part was that the horse and rider were s*keletons!* The horse was all bony and kind of a murky green color. The rider wore black boots and a top hat. Draped over his bony shoulders was a red overcoat.

Next to me, Holly gasped, but she managed to snap a couple pictures with her disposable camera. I could hear Dylan's teeth chattering. As for me, I didn't make a sound, but I could sure feel my heart beating a mile a minute!

And when the skeletal horse and its bony rider began to gallop in our direction, I knew that it was the end of the line for all of us.

8

Our terror at the sight of the horrifying skeletons charging toward us was heightened by the thundering of the horse's hooves on the wooden floor.

And worse than that . . . there was nowhere to go! No stairway leading up or down, no room to run in and hide.

Shane tried to open a door, but it was locked.

"He's coming!" Dylan shrieked.

We all scrambled, but there was nowhere to go. All of the doors around us were locked . . . and there was no way we were going to try and make it around the oncoming horse and rider and run for the stairs!

We were trapped, and the horrible apparition was getting closer and closer by the second.

We backed up against the end of the hall, against the double doors. The floor was shaking from the pounding hooves. Pictures on the wall trembled, and doorknobs rattled. We were all screaming and yelling.

And the bizarre horse and its menacing, wicked rider kept coming, faster, closer.

"He's going to run right into us!" Tony cried.

At the last moment, right when the horse was only a few feet away, we dove. Holly, Dylan and I dove to the left, while Shane, Lyle, and Tony dove to the right.

The horse and rider didn't slow. Instead, they hit the double doors, slipped through— and vanished.

The sound of thundering hooves faded instantly. The pictures no longer trembled on their hooks. The doorknobs were silent. The only thing you could hear were the gasps and wheezes of six terrified kids, laying on the floor.

Dylan sniffled and rolled over. I sat up, leaning my back against the wall.

"We're getting out of here," Shane said. "Now."

No one argued.

We leapt to our feet and started to run, jogging at

first, and then broke into an all out run, only slowing down as we reached the stairs. We thundered down the steps, holding onto the guardrail. Shane was in front, followed by Lyle, then me.

Suddenly, Shane stopped. Lyle ran into him, and I ran into Lyle. Dylan hit me from behind, and I felt another thump as Holly and Tony ran into him.

And when I saw what had caused Shane to stop, I realized that getting out of the Grand Hotel wasn't going to be as easy as we thought.

9

People.

The people that we'd seen earlier had returned . . . with one chilling distinction:

They were skeletons!

Hundreds of people were standing motionless. They wore clothing, but their bony hands poked out of their sleeves. Horrid skulls stared back at us. Some of the men wore hats, some of the women still had hair.

And they were all looking at us. Before, we could tell that the people couldn't see us.

Not anymore. We could tell that they saw us just by the way they were all facing us, unmoving. Some people held teacups or a plate. One skeleton near the bottom of the stairs held a fat, unlit cigar. None of the skeletons moved, not even single inch.

"O . . . o . . . okay," Holly stuttered behind me. Her words were barely a whisper, and her voice quivered with fear. *"So . . . what do we do now?"*

"Let's get out of here," I croaked.

Dylan spoke next.

"Guys . . . I . . . I, uh . . . I don't . . . don't . . . don't want to scare you even more," he croaked, "but the . . . the . . . ha . . . ha . . . haunted horse . . . horseman is at the top . . . top of . . . of the . . . the stairs."

We all turned to see the skeletal horse and the bony rider at the top of the stairs. The horse's nostrils flared in anger.

"Well, we aren't going that way," Lyle said weakly.

"There's only one way out," Shane cried, "and that's through that door in the back!"

"Let's just hope that it takes us back to our time," I whispered.

"Let's just hope we can get there without those freaky things getting us," said Holly.

Slowly, we continued down the steps. While I was certain that the strange, skeletal figures were watching us,

I didn't see any of them move. I felt somehow that they were mad at us and wanted us to leave. Like we weren't welcome there.

When we reached the bottom of the stairs, it was everything I could do not to break into a run. The bizarre skeletons were all around us, some only a few feet away.

And as we moved, they, too, moved.

They came closer, forming columns on either side of us, watching us intently. It was as if they had formed a path for us to follow.

That's what the old man meant, I thought. *They won't let us out any other way. The only way we'll be able to leave . . . if we can leave at all . . . is through the door we came in through.*

It was a chilling thought. As we walked, the hideous figures looked on, their eye sockets empty, but still, somehow . . . .

Staring at us. Watching us.

But I kept my cool. I think it helped that I had five friends by my side, and each one of them were just as scared as I was. Without saying a word, we felt strengthened by each other and managed to stay calm.

We wove through the crowd of morbid creatures and made our way into a large dining room. Here, hundreds of people sat at tables. Some held empty glasses, some held teacups. The only thing on the plates were the remains of food: chicken and steak bones.

And none of them made a move to touch us. We knew they were watching us, but none of them tried to move toward us or hurt us.

Finally, we found the hall and the corridor that led to the door. Now, away from the crowd of skeletons, we *did* run. Our footsteps echoed down the narrow passageway, and when we reached the door Shane threw it open so hard that it banged on the wall. We scrambled inside, and Tony shut the door behind us.

"That didn't happen!" Dylan panted, shaking his head in disbelief. "That didn't happen!"

"Hey, we all saw it," I said. "I don't know what we saw, but we sure saw something."

Ahead of us, the empty hall waited. We hurried along the passageway until we came to the door that led outside.

"Man, I hope we are back where we belong," Shane said. "I don't want to go back into a place that has a bunch of bony old skeletons."

He grasped the doorknob, and pulled.

Right away, the smell of the livery stable and the

bright sunshine made me want to cheer. On top of that, the old farrier that we'd met was only a few feet away. He was working on a horse's hoof. When he saw us, he stopped.

"Well, well," he said with a kind smile. "What did you think?"

"Man . . . there are ghosts in there!" Dylan said.

"Skeletons!" Tony added. "And a ghost rider that rides on a skeleton horse!"

The old man looked astonished. "What?!?!" he said. "That's preposterous!"

"What's 'preposterous' mean?" Dylan asked.

"It means 'absurd'," Holly replied.

"Oh," Dylan said, very matter-of-factly. Then: "What's 'absurd' mean?"

"It means 'preposterous'," Tony snickered.

"No, really!" Holly reasoned, speaking to the old man. "We were just there! The stories are all true!"

"You children have a very active imagination," the old farrier said, shaking his head. "There are no ghosts in the Grand."

"It's true," Lyle said, nodding. "We saw it all. Just a few minutes ago."

"Well, then," the old man said, "I would expect that

the 'ghosts' or whatever you call them, would still be there?"

"Absolutely," I said.

"Shall we go and see?"

"What?!?!" Dylan cried. "I'm not going back in there!"

"Yeah, let's!" Holly said. "Just to prove that what we saw was real!"

"What if that horseman comes after us?" Dylan said. His eyes were wide with fright.

"Nothing's going to happen," Shane said. "We'll go back and show him. Then we'll have our proof, and we'll leave."

"Splendid," the old man said. "Shall we?" He extended his arm toward the open door.

We were going back.

Something told me that we shouldn't do this, that we'd been lucky enough already.

But something else told me that we'd be okay. We'd prove to the old farrier that the Grand Hotel was, in fact, haunted, just like the stories said.

Then we would leave. Simple as that.

But that's not what happened.

What was about to happen was something that we

never, ever, would have suspected.

10

The seven of us made our way through the narrow corridor that led to the main hallway of the Grand. I couldn't believe we were going back into the hotel.

When we reached the door that would open into the Grand, Shane hesitated.

"What's the matter?" the old man asked.

"Nothing, I guess. I guess I'm just preparing myself for what we're going to see."

And with that, Shane turned the knob and opened the door.

We walked into the hallway, and in an instant, we knew something really weird was going on. Even weirder than what we'd already been through!

There were people in the hall. Not skeletons—but people. And they were dressed in today's styles, today's fashions. Everyday people that you might see at the mall or a department store or anywhere else.

Where had the skeletons gone? What had become of the horse and rider?

"What in the world is going on?!?!" Lyle said.

Holly looked at the old man. "They were here just a few minutes ago!" she said. "Honest!"

The old man smiled, and he looked at Holly like he didn't believe her.

"Really, sir," I said. "We're not kidding. We all saw those things."

"Kids," the old man said, bending over. "No matter who you tell, no matter what you say . . . you will never, ever prove that ghosts haunt the Grand Hotel. Ever. Do you know why?"

Not one of us answered.

Finally, the old man continued. "Because," he said, "you just can't prove that ghosts exist. Nobody ever has, nobody ever will. Oh, sure, they make great stories to tell, and some people even write books about them. But no one will ever, ever prove that there are ghosts in this hotel. You people aren't the only ones who claimed to have seen ghosts in the Grand, and you won't be the last. But the fact is, you can't prove it. And another fact? I have work to do."

And with that, the old man turned and began walking away.

We didn't say a thing. We were too dumbfounded by what we had experienced . . . and what we were now experiencing . . . to say a thing.

Just before the old man reached the corridor he turned to us and spoke. He was smiling, and I'll never forget the curious look on his face.

"Just remember, children," he said with a wave of his hand. "Here at the Grand Hotel, you might see many strange, wonderful things. You might even think you see ghosts. But you will never, ever be able to prove it."

That said, the old man winked at us—and began to disappear. He didn't walk away, he didn't walk down the corridor.

He simply faded and disappeared, washed away like smoke on a windy day.

11

The next day, we all gathered in our new clubhouse to talk about what we'd been through. We had no explanations, no reasons for the things we'd seen, no idea how or why we'd experienced what we had.

Holly was a few minutes late, and she started shouting as she climbed up the rope ladder.

"Guys! You're not going to believe this! You're not going to believe this!"

A moment later her head popped up through the hole and she scrambled inside. She sat against the wall, out of breath. She'd must have rode her bike like a madwoman.

In her hand, she had a glossy yellow envelope.

"The pictures," she gasped. "I got the pictures developed!"

We all gathered around as she opened up the envelope. "You're not going to believe this," she said again as she shuffled through the pictures.

"Did the pictures come out okay?" I asked.

"Yeah," Holly replied with a nod. "But check them out."

The photos were fine . . . except for one strange exception:

None of the people that we'd seen showed up in the pictures!

"Hey," Lyle said. "The people are gone!"

"Even the skeleton horse and rider," Holly said, showing us a picture of the second floor of the hotel. The picture showed only an empty hall.

"But wait," Holly said, shuffling to the bottom of the pile. "This one is the strangest of all."

Holly held up the picture for all of us to see. It was the one that had been taken in the livery stable, with the six of us posing with the old man and the horse. The picture came out very clear . . . but the old man was gone!

"Holy grass snakes!" Shane said, taking the photo from Holly's hand. He examined it closely. "He's gone!"

he said. "It's like he was never there!"

We all shuddered. What a weird, weird adventure that had been.

"Maybe it's like he said," I offered.

"Like who said?" Dylan asked.

"The old man—or ghost, or whatever he was. Maybe the existence of ghosts just can't be proven."

"But what about the graveyard near Devil's Ridge?" Tony asked. "We all know that was super-freaky." Not long ago we'd had an experience that none of us could ever explain . . . but we knew we'd seen a ghost near Devil's Ridge.

"Well," Shane said, "whatever happened at Devil's Ridge was nothing compared to what we saw at the Grand Hotel."

We talked for a long time about ghosts and things that we couldn't understand. Sometimes, if you try to remember really hard, you begin to think you saw things that you really didn't see.

But that wasn't the case this time. We'd all experienced the same thing. We all saw the horrifying horse and rider, and all of the skeletons looking at us. We couldn't understand it, but we knew what we'd seen.

And so . . . we moved on. The summer wasn't over

yet, and there were still lots of things we wanted to do.

"I say we go explore that underwater tunnel some more," Shane said. "Let's go through it again, and go into Lake Huron."

"Yeah," Tony said sarcastically. "Let's just not surface in the middle of the shipping lane again."

We discussed different ideas, and we decided that we'd set out on a fishing expedition. Which, of course, wouldn't really be an 'expedition'. We would use the Bunker's pontoon boat and moor it over the rock pile in front of Puckett Park. Not many people know about the spot, and it's a great place to fish.

Our expedition wouldn't go as planned.

What would happen was something that I thought could only happen in our worst nightmares. Something that was far more horrifying than seeing ghosts, or being threatened by the Martin brothers.

It was more horrifying . . . because it was real. And for the first time ever, all six of us in the Adventure Club were about to find ourselves not only battling to fix a problem—we found ourselves in a battle to save our lives.

FIRESTORM

1

Sometimes things happen that you have little or no control over. There's not a lot you can do to change these things, and the only thing you can do is the best you can with what you have.

It was a beautiful summer day in Great Bear Heart. It had been really hot for weeks. Puckett Lake was filled with boaters and swimmers, and the local park was clogged with the usual locals. Sun glittered and danced like shards of glass on the lake. Kids played on the swings, and adults chatted at picnic tables while they sipped iced tea. A yellow labrador was chasing a Frisbee into the lake, returning the toy to its owner on shore, only to be tossed out again.

Sure enough, it was a day just like the day before, and the day before that one. It hadn't rained in a long time, and the air was dry as a bone. I saw on television that the Forest Service was ordering people not to burn anything outside . . . no campfires, burn barrels . . . nothing.

Which seemed pretty smart, considering how dry it was. It would be too easy for a fire to get out of control.

Our plan for this particular day was to dig up some worms, and then go fishing. Straight out from Puckett Park in the lake is an old rock pile. Actually, it's the remains of a huge dock that used to stretch out into the lake from an old hotel that has been long gone. The rock pile is a habitat for fish—bass, pike, bluegill, but mainly, rock bass—and is some of the best fishing around. One day, we caught over one hundred rock bass!

I found a shovel in the garage, and I carried it over to Holly O'Mara's house. She, too, had a shovel, and we hiked out to our new clubhouse deep in the woods. Dollar the cat followed closely at our heels. Rarely did Holly go anywhere without that cat. I must admit, we were all kind of attached to the animal. Dollar was pretty cute, and as loyal as a good friend, which I thought was kind of odd. Most of the cats I knew were pretty independent and did what they wanted to do, despite what their owner wanted.

We met up with Shane along the way. We were walking, and Shane rode up behind us on his bike.

"Check this out," Shane said. On his hip, attached to his belt, was a hatchet. The hatchet was in a leather case so the blade was covered. Shane unsnapped it and held up the tool.

"I got it at a garage sale for fifty cents!" he exclaimed proudly. "Can you believe it?!?!"

"Wow," Holly said. "It looks brand new."

"It is, practically," Shane said.

"Man, you always find the cool stuff," I said.

Shane returned the hatchet to its case on his belt. "I'll meet you guys at the clubhouse," he said, and he rode off.

"Sure is hot," I said, wiping a film of perspiration from my forehead.

"I think we ought to go swimming instead of fishing," Holly replied.

"We can do both," I said. "It's still early in the day. After we get our worms, we can go for a swim before we go fishing. Besides . . . the fishing won't be very good until the evening, when it gets a little cooler."

At the clubhouse, Shane, Lyle, and Tony were already there. We waited around for Dylan, who, as usual, was fifteen minutes late, and he had all kinds of excuses about why he couldn't make it on time.

"Honest, guys," he said. "My mom made me clean my room. Then I had to take the trash to the dumpster, and then I had to—"

"Can it, Dylan," Shane said. "It doesn't matter. Let's just get going."

"Let's head over to the swamp where the ground is wetter," Lyle said. "Everything around here is too dry. We should be able to find a lot of worms over there."

That sounded like a good idea, so we scrambled out of our clubhouse and down the rope ladder. Tony Gritter and Dylan Bunker had each brought a shovel, and Lyle Haywood brought a pail to put the worms in. Holly, Dylan, Tony and I carried the shovels over our shoulders as we walked, and I couldn't help but think of the seven dwarfs heading off to work.

The swamp wasn't very far, but soon, we were all soaked with sweat. The sun beat down mercilessly, and if it wasn't for a stiff wind that had begun to blow, I think we all would have cooked like Thanksgiving turkeys.

But we had another problem to deal with, and it had

nothing to do with the weather.

It had to do with the Martin brothers.

2

We were almost to the swamp when suddenly, we heard a loud *pop!* high above us. It sounded like a firecracker.

We stopped and looked up, squinting in the late morning sun.

"What was that?" Dylan asked. His hand was pressed to his forehead, shading his eyes from the hot sun as he gazed into the sky.

We couldn't see anything.

"Sounded like a firecracker," Tony said.

When we heard nothing more, we continued our hike. A few minutes later, we heard another sound. It was a fizzling hiss that faded away. Then, once again, a loud *pop!* came from high above.

"I know what *that* is," Lyle said confidently. "That's a bottle rocket."

"Who would be shooting off bottle rockets way out here?" I asked.

"I'll give you three guesses," Holly replied, and we all knew who she meant. There were only three people we could think of that would be shooting off bottle rockets in the middle of the forest.

Gary, Larry, and Terry.

The Martin brothers.

They were at the edge of the swamp, where a wide-open field of tall, dry grass opens up. They spotted us the same time we spotted them.

"Hey, it's the six losers!" Gary shouted. Larry had just lit another bottle rocket and he jumped back. The needle-like device shot up into the air with a hiss, then exploded high in the sky.

"It's the Three Stooges," Tony called back.

"Tony!" Holly hissed. She didn't want any trouble with the Martins. None of us did, really.

Terry lit a bottle rocket and it shot up into the sky.

"Get outta here," Larry said. "Can't you see we're busy?"

Tony was going to say something but Shane stopped him.

"Just leave them alone," he whispered, and we kept walking. Fortunately, they didn't say anything else. After we passed, we could still hear the pops high in the air. Every so often one of the Martins would cheer.

"They shouldn't be messing around with those things," Holly said, "especially out in the woods."

"Hey, that's the Martin brothers for you," I said. "They aren't very bright to begin with."

We found a place near the edge of the swamp. I started to dig, and found the ground to be black, soggy, and wet. I found three worms on my first shovel full of dirt.

"Hey, this is a good spot," I said, and I snatched up the worms and placed them in the pail that Lyle had brought.

"Toss some dirt in that bucket for the worms," Lyle said, and I dumped a shovelful into the pail.

"Hey, I found a nightcrawler!" Dylan exclaimed, holding up a long, pencil-sized worm. It was squirming like crazy as he dropped it in the pail.

Unfortunately, we didn't find many more worms, and after about fifteen minutes, we gave up and decided to head to another spot. Holly picked up her shovel and paused. She had a curious look on her face.

"What?" I asked. "What's the matter?"

She shook her head. "Nothing, I guess," she replied, and that was all she said. But she had a curious, worried look on her face.

"Let's follow the swamp on the other side of Devil's Ridge," Shane said. "We might have better luck over there."

We hadn't heard any more bottle rockets exploding in the past few minutes, so we figured that the Martin brothers had left, which made all of us glad. The less we saw of them, the better.

We hiked along the edge of the swamp. My shirt was soaked with sweat and it clung to my skin. Sweat dripped into my right eye, and man, did it sting! I winced and closed my eyes for a moment until the pain subsided.

Holly stopped suddenly, a look of real concern on her face. We all stopped.

"What is it?" Lyle asked.

"I smell smoke," she said, alarmed. She was carrying her shovel over her shoulder. With the other arm, she held Dollar. The kitten had fallen asleep.

The rest of us sniffed the air. I didn't smell anything.

"Are you sure?" Tony asked.

Holly nodded. "I thought I smelled it back there a ways, but I thought I was imagining things. I'm sure of it now."

We looked around.

"I don't see anything," Shane said. "Maybe because it's so hot—"

"Shane, I smell smoke," Holly insisted. "I *know* I do."

"Okay, whatever," he said.

Suddenly Lyle gasped and pointed to the other side of the field. A flicker of yellow danced between the thick branches.

"Fire!" Lyle shrieked.

It wasn't a very big fire, and we sprang toward it to try and stop the growing flames. Hopefully, we could stop the fire before it spread. With everything as dry as it was, the whole woods could go up in flames in no time.

Unfortunately, we would soon find ourselves in a situation that was far beyond our control.

3

We raced across the field. Four of us had shovels, and we would have to use them to put out the fire.

"The Martin brothers and their bottle rockets!" Tony shouted as we ran. *"They started the fire! They should never have been out here with those things!"*

When we reached the other side of the field, we knew we had our work cut out for us. The fire was burning the dry grass, sending wisps of gray smoke into the air. Flames had also ignited the lower limbs of a tree, and we knew that if they spread into other trees, there would be no stopping the fire.

Shane knew what he had to do. He unsnapped his

hatchet and went to work at the base of the tree, chopping at the trunk.

"Good thinking!" Lyle exclaimed. "Chop down the tree before the flames get too high!"

The four of us with shovels—Holly, Dylan, Tony and I—went to work battling the blaze in the grass. We patted out the flames and covered the fire with dirt. It wasn't very easy. The grass was so dry that flames kept popping back up even after we thought they had been extinguished. Holly placed Dollar on a nearby log, and the kitten sat quietly, watching in a sort of mild amusement. The cat looked as if nothing was wrong at all, and probably wondered why us silly humans were scurrying about so frantically.

"Man, the Martins are in for it this time!" I shouted as I worked.

"They're going to be in a lot of trouble for this!" Dylan said.

"Okay, she's coming down!" Shane warned. "Watch out! Watch out!"

We dashed to the side as the tree came down. Flames had spread to the higher branches, but so far, the fire hadn't ignited any more trees.

"Get those flames out!" Shane ordered, and we ran up to the fallen tree and began pounding at the flames with the blades of our shovels. Shane worked at chopping off burning limbs with his hatchet, while Lyle was busy stomping out the smaller flames in the grass with his shoes, since he didn't have a shovel.

Finally, the flames were extinguished. The ground smoked, however, and we knew that at any moment the fire could flare up again. We continued working, digging into the dirt and piling it on top of the smoldering grass.

"We have to get help," Lyle said. "The fire department is going to have to come to make sure this thing is completely out. Otherwise, it might start up again."

"Well, some of us are going to have to stay to keep an eye on it, then," Shane said. His face was sweaty and dirty, and so was everyone else's. Our clothing was filthy.

"I'll stay," Tony said.

"Yeah, me, too," I replied, leaning on my shovel.

"Holly and I'll go," Lyle said. "We'll go get the fire department and lead them back here."

"While you're at it, make sure you tell them who started the fire," Tony growled.

"Oh, man," Dylan said. He sounded scared. "Oh, man. Oh, man."

"What?" I asked.

He pointed. "I don't think you guys are going anywhere. Look!"

It had to be ninety-five degrees in the sun, but a cold dagger shot down my spine and chilled my entire body.

In front of us, on the other side of the field, flames began to lick high into the air.

To the west, in another spot altogether, flames

suddenly sprouted.

And to the east, still more flames were growing, slithering up pine trees like yellow snakes.

The entire forest around us was on fire.

4

"We've got to get out of here!" Holly exclaimed. She snapped up Dollar into her arms. "There is fire all around us!"

"We can't go back the way we came!" Shane said. "It's all on fire!"

"We're going to have to loop around the north! " Lyle said. "If we can loop around, we can get back to the Mail Route road!"

By now, plumes of smoke were clouding the sky. We were at the edge of the field, and it seemed like the fire was everywhere. I couldn't believe how fast it was spreading. Flames leapt thirty feet into the air, and we could hear the roaring blazes even from where we were.

"Well, if we're going to get out of here, we'd better do it now," I said. "The whole forest is going to go up in flames!"

"Lyle!" Holly exclaimed. "Take my shovel! I have to carry Dollar!"

Lyle grabbed Holly's shovel, and the six of us sprang. We headed north, where the flames were thinner.

"You know what happened?" Shane said, huffing and puffing as we ran through the field. "I'll bet those bottle rockets that the Martin brothers were shooting off started all of these fires! It's so dry that when the spent rockets hit the ground, they were still hot enough to start a fire!"

"There might be four or five different fires!" Holly gasped. "They could have all started in different places, at almost the exact same time!"

"They are really going to get it for this!" Dylan said. "Just wait until we get back to town!"

"I'll bet they get arrested!" Tony said. "I hope Officer Hulburt locks them in the slammer and throws away the key!"

We reached the forest and started winding through the trees. Here, there was no trail, so the going was really tough. We had to zig-zag around trees and branches. Suddenly, I spotted flames ahead of us.

"Stop!" I cried, and we huffed to a halt.

Up ahead was a wall of fire, fueled by closely-knit pine trees.

"End of the road," Shane said. "Come on! Let's go this way!"

We followed Shane as we worked our way around the blaze. It was impossible to tell just how many fires were burning, or where the fire began and ended.

The smoke became thicker. I was aware of it as we ran across the field, but here, in the dense forest, it was heavier. We were all hacking and coughing, trying to keep the smoke out of our lungs.

Once again, we came upon another portion of the forest that was burning.

"Okay, so that didn't work," Shane said. "Let's head around this way!"

We took off in the only direction we could, hoping that we wouldn't run into more fires. The smoke began to thin out a little, and we were hopeful that we were headed in the right direction.

We weren't. We were headed right into the very center of the growing fires—we just didn't know it yet.

5

There were three things I didn't like about the situation we were in.

Number one, the forest was so thick that we couldn't run anymore. Branches smacked at our faces, and we had to duck around limbs and skirt around trees and brush.

Number two, I wasn't really sure where we were. Most of us in the Adventure Club were pretty familiar with the forest around Great Bear Heart, but now we were turned around and confused. I knew from the position of the sun that we were headed west, but that was all I knew. And west wouldn't take us back to town.

Somehow, we were going to have to angle north and cut back over to get back to Great Bear Heart.

And number three, we had no idea where the fires were headed. We didn't know if we were heading into a fire, or away from it.

Smoke clouded the sky, and everything took on a dirty yellow cast. I thought I heard an airplane, but I couldn't see it.

"Does anyone hear that?" Shane asked.

"It sounds like a plane," Holly said. We had stopped walking, and we were all looking up into the dirty, smoke-filled sky.

"I'm sure that the fires have been reported by now," Lyle said. "That's probably one of the spotter planes."

"Let's hope he spots us," I said.

We started off again, moving as fast as we could, considering the thick brush we had to go through. Again, we came across an area of fire and had to change our direction.

Suddenly, we came to a field. I'd been here before, but it had been a long time. I knew that we were nearly a mile from Great Bear Heart.

"The town is that way," I pointed. However, the direction I was pointing was consumed by fire.

"At least there is a field here," Dylan said. "If we stay in the field, we can stay away from the forest, where the fire is burning."

"Only for the time being," Lyle said. "The fires are moving so fast that we'd never be able to outrun a grass fire. And this field is nothing but dry grass. If it catches fire, it will burn like gasoline!"

For the first time, I really started to get worried. I mean, it was scary seeing all of those fires popping up all around . . . but I thought that all we would have to do is walk around them, and we would be home and out of danger.

Now, however, it appeared that the fires were all around us . . . and there might not be a way out.

"We have one big problem," Shane said as he looked around the field. Fires seemed to be everywhere. "These fires are moving fast, and when they come together, they're just getting bigger. There's a chance that all of these fires might merge together into one huge fire. And if that happens . . . ."

He stopped speaking, and we were all silent, watching the distant flames and the smoke billowing up into the sky. Finally, Holly spoke.

"If that happens," she said quietly, "it'll never be

stopped. It will wipe out the whole town."

Her words felt like weights attached to my soul. I couldn't even begin to imagine the town of Great Bear Heart on fire. People would lose their homes and businesses—or worse.

And I couldn't imagine that at all.

"All right," Shane said. His glance traveled to each one of us. "We're getting out of here. We're going to use our heads, we aren't going to panic. We're going to get through this."

It was nice of him to say, but I had my doubts. I was scared. We all were.

Tony pointed. "Over there," he said. "The fire has already been through that area. We might be able to get through there and make it back to town."

"Tony's right," Lyle said. "Besides . . . we don't have any idea where we might run into more fire. If we can find some places where the fire has already been through, we might be able to make it back."

"Then let's go," I said. "The quicker we get out of here, the better."

In the distance, we could hear sirens blaring. It was comforting to know that people were fighting the fire, but we still had our own problems to deal with.

We hiked across the field and came to a swamp. The fire hadn't come this far, but when I turned around, I could see flames licking high into the air—and the wind was blowing them in our direction.

"Through the swamp," Shane said. "If we can make it through the swamp, we'll be at the south end of Devil's Ridge. Depending on where the fire is, we might be able to follow the ridge back around and into town."

A little bit about Devil's Ridge:

It's a barren hill west of Great Bear Heart. It runs east and west for about a quarter of a mile. At the north end of the ridge, the hill is almost all rock, and there is a jagged cliff right at the end. There's a tunnel at the mouth of the ledge that leads all the way back to Great Bear Heart. At the bottom of the slope is an old cemetery. A lot of people are spooked by the graveyard, so Devil's Ridge doesn't have many visitors.

All around us, smoke filled the sky. We could hear the buzzing of a plane, but there was so much smoke that we couldn't see it. We knew that the pilot probably couldn't see us, either.

"You know," I said, as we struggled through the swamp, "if we make it to Devil's Ridge, maybe we could climb through the tunnel back to Great Bear Heart."

Lyle's eyes widened. "You're right, Parker! We could do it! It'll be tough to get into the entrance of the tunnel, but it just might work!"

Hope blossomed. Not a lot, but a tiny bit. From what we could see, Devil's Ridge wasn't on fire. If we made it that far, our chances would be a lot better. Maybe things would work out, after all.

But when we emerged from the swamp, we got a good look around. For the first time, we could see that Shane was right. The fires had merged. They had merged into one big firestorm . . . and we were downwind.

A hurricane of fire was coming straight for us.

6

Seeing those giant, yellow and red tongues licking up into the sky, curling and seething, was like a nightmare. Dark plumes of smoke were pushed upward, boiling and churning, devouring what had once been a crystal-blue sky.

Flames were everywhere around us, and it was impossible to see Devil's Ridge. We knew approximately where it was, but in all the smoke and flame it was hard to tell for sure.

One thing was certain: the flames were rapidly closing in on us. We'd be forced to move . . . or else.

"Come on!" Shane cried, and we took off after him.

All around us, trees were burning. Smoke filled my lungs and I gasped for air. Still, we pressed on. A burning tree fell right in front of us, crashing to the ground and exploding in a blistering shower of orange sparks. The intense heat from the fire was awful. The heat from the sun earlier in the morning was *nothing* like what it felt as we made our way through the forest.

Again, we heard the plane, but we couldn't see it. We could still hear sirens, but they sounded distant, drowned by the roaring blaze.

Finally, a break. We came to a place that hadn't yet been charred by fire, and we stopped to get some air.

And that's where it happened.

Holly had been carrying Dollar in her arms. The kitten had been calm and quiet through everything so far, but something must have spooked it. In a flash, it leapt from Holly's arms and landed on the ground.

"Dollar!" Holly shouted as the kitten scampered off. *"Dollar! Stop! Please! Stop!"*

It was too late. The kitten bounded away and never looked back, disappearing into a fog of smoke and ash.

"Holly! No!" I screamed.

But it was too late. There was no way that Holly was going to leave the cat to fend for itself in the fire. That would mean certain death for the animal.

And Holly just wasn't going to let that happen. Before we could stop her, she had vanished in the smoke and flames.

Holly O'Mara—probably my best friend in the whole world—was gone.

7

We were stunned.

The fire roared around us. Tree trunks were exploding in the intense heat. Smoke twisted like crazed vipers.

And Holly was gone. She had feared for Dollar's life, and now, she, too, was—

I couldn't bear to think about it. Tears welled up in my eyes. Dylan started crying.

"Holly," Shane whispered, choking back a sob. *"Holly . . . ."*

And I don't know exactly how I made the decision. I don't know how Lyle, Tony, Shane, or Dylan came to the same decision, at the same time, without even speaking.

But we did.

We were going to survive. We were getting out of this fire.

But not without Holly.

And suddenly, the five of us were running, fearless, darting around burning trees and brush. Much of the earth was charred, blackened ash, and I could feel the heat through my sneakers. Smoke burned my eyes, but I wouldn't close them. If I closed them, I wouldn't be able to see Holly.

"Holly!" I screamed at the top of my lungs. Dylan, Lyle, Shane and Tony called out, too. We searched the dense smoke for any sign of our friend.

Suddenly, through the grimy haze, I caught a movement.

"Over there!" I shouted. *"I saw something!"*

We charged through the fire and debris and found—

Holly!

She was crouched on the ground, gasping for breath. Dollar was safely in her arms.

"Holly!" I shrieked, running up to her. She looked up. Her face was black from soot, and her dark hair was all tangled and knotted. She had a scrape on her neck, and there was a little bit of blood on her right hand.

But she was alive. She was all right.

I grabbed her by the hand and helped her up.

"Now we're getting out of here!" I said. "We're getting out of here and we're going home!"

"This way!" Shane said, taking charge, and I held Holly's hand as we charged after him. It was up to Shane now. He was our club president, our leader. We had to put our trust in him. All of it.

Smoke filled our lungs, and the pain was awful. We all coughed and spluttered. The heat was unbearable. Fire was all around, above us, on the ground. No matter which direction we went, we were surrounded by flames or charred embers.

And suddenly—

One of the most glorious, wonderful sights I think I had ever seen:

An entire field that hadn't been scorched. Long blades of grass whipped in the fire-fueled wind. But so far, Devil's Ridge hadn't burned.

Our problem was that the fire had looped around the ridge, cutting off any other escape route. No matter how we looked at it, we were trapped on Devil's Ridge . . . and an enormous firestorm was rapidly approaching.

And if the fire jumped the ridge, nothing would stop it from reaching Great Bear Heart. Even the fire fighters wouldn't be able to stop it in time. The tiny town on Puckett Lake would be wiped out.

"Okay, here's what we're going to do," Shane said. "We're going to dig a trench at the bottom of the ridge, all the way across."

"What?!?!" Tony cried. "Let's just climb up to the tunnel and crawl to town!"

"We still have time. We're going to be safe, I promise. But we have a chance to stop the main part of the fire . . . or at least slow it down . . . before it reaches Great Bear Heart. Look around! It's all grass! The ridge is mostly rock. If we can create a fire break, maybe that'll stop the fire from leaping the ridge and continuing on into town."

"But Shane . . . shouldn't we get out of here while we still have a chance to make it back to town?" Tony reasoned.

"Tony . . . if we don't at least *try* to slow this fire down, we might not have a town to go back to."

Shane was right. We knew he was.

"Okay, let's vote," he said. "Do we leave now, or do

we stay and dig a trench? Even if we dig the trench, we'll still have time to get to the tunnel before the fire gets here." He looked at each of us. "All in favor of staying?"

And you know what? The first person to raise his hand was Dylan Bunker. I couldn't believe it. Ten minutes ago he had been scared out of his wits . . . now, he was the first to volunteer to fight the fire.

"I say we stay and dig," he said.

The rest of us raised our hands.

"Motion passed," Shane said. "We stay and fight. We have four shovels. Holly . . . you climb to the top of the ridge and keep an eye on the fire. Every sixty seconds, shout down to us and let us know where it is."

"Got it," Holly said.

Shane removed his hatchet from it's sheath and he handed it to Lyle. "Lyle, you clear any brush you see near the bottom of the ridge. The rest of us will dig. If anybody gets tired, switch jobs with Lyle. Everybody ready?"

We all nodded. Without speaking, we went to work. Holly, still cradling Dollar in her arms, climbed to the top of Devil's Ridge.

"I can see fire trucks way over on another hill!" she

shouted down to us. That was good news. That meant that crews had been able to get into the woods and were battling the blaze before it reached any of the outlying houses.

And we dug. And dug. And dug. A straight line, two feet wide, all along the bottom of Devil's Ridge. Lyle picked up logs and branches—anything that could catch fire—and hauled them back from our fire break. He used Shane's hatchet to chop up the bigger pieces to make them easier to move. Our intent was to create a long line where the fire had nothing to burn.

Gray ash began to fall on us like snow, and the wind grew hotter.

"It's on the other side of the swamp!" Holly called down.

"We've got to finish up!" Shane ordered. "Faster! Once that swamp catches fire, it's going to burn like paper!"

We worked frantically, digging the trench deeper, wider, farther. My muscles ached, and sweat streamed down my face.

Holly's voice suddenly echoed down. "The swamp's on fire!" she shouted with increased urgency. "Guys! It's burning really fast!"

I turned and gasped. Holly was right. The fire wasn't just burning the swamp . . . it was eating it alive.

"Let's get out of here!" Tony shouted, and the five of us dropped our shovels and scrambled up the ridge where Holly waited.

I turned around, and what I saw was a monster. A giant, yellow and orange monster, spewing black and gray smoke high into the air. Fire, like the jaws and teeth of some wicked beast, was gobbling up trees and brush. Far to the north, above the tree line, I could see a big, red, four-wheel-drive fire truck on a hill.

"Let's go!" Shane said. "Let's get in that tunnel and get back to town!"

"What about our shovels?" Dylan asked.

Shane shook his head. "We'll have to leave them behind. There's no way we'll be able to crawl through the tunnel with them."

Getting into the tunnel was harder than we thought. The entrance is below the ledge, and we had to swing our legs over the edge and almost dangle off the cliff to get inside. Tony went first, and he helped Holly. Then I went, followed by Dylan, Lyle and Shane.

Now, all we had to do was follow the tunnel underground to Great Bear Heart. It comes out right beneath the Great Bear Heart Public Library. Boy! Mrs. Norberg, the librarian, sure was in for a surprise!

"We've got one problem," Lyle said.

"What's that?" Shane asked.

"We don't have a light. We won't be able to see a thing."

"Then we'll go slow," Shane said.

"But what if the fire leaps the fire break?" Dylan asked. "Won't the tunnel get filled up with smoke?"

"Dylan is right," Holly said. "Let's stop talking and

get moving."

Would we really make it back to Great Bear Heart?

Only time would tell . . . but time wasn't something that we had a lot of.

8

The tunnel was so narrow that we had to travel single-file and crawl on our hands and knees. The light from the opening of the tunnel disappeared quickly, and I must admit that I was pretty nervous. Not only were we cramped in a rocky tunnel on our hands and knees, but we couldn't see a single thing. Shane was in the lead, and he was finding his way by reaching his hands out in front of him.

"Now I know how ants feel," Tony said, which caused us all to laugh. Not a lot, but a little, which was kind of nice. There hadn't been anything to laugh about all day.

Thankfully, the farther we went, the tunnel became wider and taller. Soon, we were able to stand up, but we had to stoop over.

"I hope we don't run into any bats in here," I heard Holly say. Tony snickered.

"Yeah, that would be just our luck," Lyle said.

After a few hundred feet of really uncomfortable walking, we were able to continue without stooping over—but we still had to go slow. The ground beneath us was rugged and rocky, and we stumbled a lot. With every step, however, we were feeling more and more confident that we would make it out.

Until we started to smell smoke.

We all caught a whiff of it at the same time, and there was no mistake what it was.

"We've got to move faster!" Shane said. "Move faster, but be careful!"

"I can't see a single thing," Dylan complained.

"None of us can," I said. "Let's just stay together and get out of here."

We would still have a problem trying to get out of the tunnel. The entrance of the tunnel is behind a hidden door at the Great Bear Heart Public Library. There's a bookshelf against the door, and most people don't know that it's there.

Suddenly, a faint light appeared, just a single, horizontal bar about three feet long.

"Look!" Dylan exclaimed. "It's the door to the library! It's the door to the library!"

Sure enough, light was streaming through the bottom of the door. It didn't provide enough illumination to see, but that didn't matter. What mattered was that we knew that we were almost home.

"Careful," I said. "Remember: there are steps we have to go up."

"Parker's right," Shane said. "Watch your step." The old boards creaked and moaned as we slowly shuffled up the stairs. When we reached the top, Shane pounded on the door.

"Mrs. Norberg?" he called out. "Mrs. Norberg? It's me . . . Shane Mitchell."

No answer.

Shane pounded again. "Mrs. Norberg?"

"I don't think anyone is here," Lyle said.

Shane turned the doorknob and pushed slowly. A trickle of light spilled in.

"Problem is," Shane said with a wince, "this bookshelf is right against the door."

"I'll help," Tony said, and he stepped up next to Shane. The two of them pushed.

"Slow," Shane said. "Otherwise we're going to knock the whole thing—"

CRASH!

"Too late," Holly said.

Dylan giggled, and so did Holly. Then I started laughing, and finally Tony, Lyle, and Shane. In light of everything that had happened, knocking over a bookshelf was the least of our problems.

Shane pushed the door the rest of the way open. Books were scattered all over the floor, and the bookshelf was on its side. We hastily stood the shelf up and picked up the books. We didn't put them back in the right order, but I didn't think Mrs. Norberg would be too upset, considering the circumstances.

"Let's find out what's going on!" I said. We slipped out the back door and locked it behind us.

Great Bear Heart looked like a ghost town. A thick, brown haze hung in the air, discoloring the sun. Puckett Park was empty.

"Where is everybody?" Dylan asked.

"They evacuated the town, I bet," Lyle said. "That fire must have jumped our fire break. It's probably headed our way!"

Not again!

"Let's see if we can find anyone," Holly said, and we walked onto the deserted, single main street that wound through town.

Suddenly, coming up over the hill, was a police car! Its lights were flashing and its siren was wailing. We stepped onto the shoulder of the road to let it pass, but it didn't. It screeched to a halt right in front of us.

We were either being saved . . . or we were in a lot of trouble.

9

A door opened, I saw a flash of brown uniform—

And Officer Hulburt stepped out!

"Man, are we glad to see you!" Shane said.

"Likewise," Officer Hulburt said, he extended his hand to Shane, and Shane grasped it. Officer Hulburt shook hands with all of us. He had a big smile on his face. "It's my honor and pleasure," he said, "to shake the hands of the bravest kids I have ever met. The kids who single-handedly saved Great Bear Heart."

"What?!" I exclaimed.

"That's right," Officer Hulburt replied with a nod. "That fire break you dug at Devil's Ridge stopped the fire just long enough for the Forest Service to get in with their heavy machinery. They were on a hill about a half-mile away when one of the firefighters spotted you guys. Their crews reached Devil's Ridge just as the flames were igniting the grass. They were able to slow the fire just as it began to leap over the ridge. It's not out yet, but it's no longer a threat to the town."

"Is that why no one is here?" Holly asked, looking around.

Officer Hulburt nodded. "When we knew that the town was in danger, we evacuated everyone. We've given the 'all clear' signal, so I imagine folks will be coming back soon. But I must say . . . all of your parents are worried sick. I just radioed back to get the message to them that you're all okay. Dirty . . . but okay. "

We all looked at our reflections in the windows of Officer Hulburt's patrol car. We didn't even look like us! Our skin was blackened by ash and soot, and so was our clothing. I was sure my jeans were ruined, and I figured I'd have to scrub for weeks and weeks to get the grime off my skin!

Another vehicle appeared over the hill. It was a bright red pickup truck. It slowed to a stop, and the driver got out. He was wearing a dark green uniform.

"You kids could have been killed up there," he said sternly. He crossed his arms and said nothing more.

"But we weren't," Dylan said sheepishly.

The man reached into his truck and pulled out what looked to be burned sparklers.

"We found some of these in the forest," he said. "It's how the fire started. Any idea who they belong to?"

The bottle rockets! They'd found the burned bottle rockets in the forest!

"Well, guys?" Officer Hulburt said. "Any ideas?"

"Yeah," Tony sneered. "Three ideas."

"And six witnesses," I said.

"You guys are sure?"

We all nodded. "You bet," Holly said.

"That's what I wanted to hear," the man said gruffly. "I know exactly where we can pick those boys up. That's who we suspected all along." He got back into his truck, then looked at us. "I don't know who you kids are, but that was a very brave thing you did back there. Risky . . . but brave. You can work my fire line with my crew any time." Then he nodded and sped away.

"Jeepers," Dylan said. "I sure wouldn't want to be in the Martin's shoes right now."

Officer Hulburt smiled. "See?" he said. "You guys

are heroes."

We didn't say a thing. I think we were all too tired.

"Look," Officer Hulburt said, "I've still got a lot of work to do, and you need to get cleaned up and find your folks. People should be returning to town any minute now. You kids need anything? Any of you hurt?"

We all shook our heads. Holly had a cut on her hand and it had bled a little, and she had a big scratch on her neck, but she said she was okay.

And when Officer Hulburt drove off, we all breathed a sigh of relief.

Heroes.

We really didn't feel like it. Or maybe it hadn't sunk in yet.

Regardless, we certainly weren't prepared for what would happen in the days that followed.

10

The fire was completely contained by the following morning. Still, a thick haze of smoke hung over the town. Some people wore white masks when they went outdoors.

And everywhere I went, people that I didn't even know came up to me. They shook my hand, and told me how thankful they were for what my friends and I had done. I told them that it was nothing, but they said that the six of us were heroes.

My mom and dad were proud, too. When they got home that night, Mom hugged me and cried. Dad gave me a hug and told me that he'd heard about how we made that fire break and slowed the fire enough for the crews to stop it from reaching the town. He wanted me to tell Mom and him all about how we did it.

The Martins, as you can imagine, were in BIG trouble. They didn't get arrested, but the police were at their house for a long time, and so were some members of the Forest Service.

Luckily, the fire didn't destroy any homes, which the man on TV said was a miracle. The only building that burned was Mr. Beansworth's old barn—what was left of it after we'd taken the wood we needed for our new clubhouse.

Which was another thing that was spared. The fire came within a hundred feet of the tree where we'd built the fort, but that was it.

Luck had really been on our side that day.

Norm Beeblemeyer, a local reporter, did an article for the *Great Bear Heart Times* and put a picture of all six of us on the front page. The caption beneath it read: *HEROES!*

Ed Skinner, the town mayor, made a proclamation that, every year on the anniversary of the forest fire, it would be 'Adventure Club' day. He gave us each a certificate of appreciation.

We were on television, too. A crew came and set up their equipment in the park, and we sat at a picnic table and answered questions. They wanted to see our clubhouse, so they packed up all their equipment and hiked back into the woods. They didn't want to climb up the rope ladder, so they filmed us as we scrambled up to our tree fort.

All in all, things really turned out cool. Mrs. Peterson, who owns and runs *The Kona* café, wanted to do something for us. She said she would like to give us each a free breakfast as a thank you for saving the town, which we thought was really nice.

And it was there, at *The Kona* café, that we made an incredible discovery.

THE
SECRET
OF
THE
ANCIENT
TOTEM

1

Three days after the fire, the six of us gathered at *The Kona* to have breakfast. We sat at a big round table in front of an old totem pole that was made long before the restaurant was built. Now the totem pole is used as a place to hang your coat at the restaurant.

Everywhere we went, there were still a lot of people that we didn't know coming up and talking to us, thanking us for what we did. And I must admit—we were really proud. Not just of what *we* did, but of Shane's quick thinking. He was the one who had the foresight to think about making that fire break.

"I vote that we elect Shane Mitchell as president of

the Adventure Club for life," Lyle said, raising his hand. The rest of us did the same, and Shane just shook his head and laughed.

Mrs. Peterson brought us glasses of orange juice and said that we could order anything we wanted from the menu. I ordered bacon and eggs, my favorite.

"Well, what's our next gig?" Tony asked.

"I think we've done about enough for one summer," Lyle said with a grin. "I'd bet not many kids get to do the things we do."

"Let's take out the *Independence* again!" Dylan exclaimed.

"Oh, we'll do that for sure," Shane replied.

Holly had brought Dollar with her. The kitten was sleeping in the pocket of her sweatshirt. When Mrs. Peterson brought our food, Dollar woke up. Holly placed the cat on her lap.

We ate, talked, and laughed. Mrs. Peterson brought more orange juice, and that reminded me of the time when we'd set up a roadside diner and sold food and juice to make extra money. It sure would be fun to do that again.

Dollar leapt from Holly's lap and wandered around. Holly was going to scoop him up, but Mrs. Peterson said that it was okay, and even put out a small bowl of milk for him.

And we kept talking about ideas, trying to come up with more cool things to do. Dylan and I wanted to build another flying machine like we had earlier in the year. Holly thought it would be cool to explore the old schoolhouse a few blocks away. It's been boarded up for years, and is rumored to be haunted. None of us were very anxious to have another experience with ghosts just yet. Tony wanted us all to enter the annual Puckett Lake fishing derby. He said he was sure we would win, and there was a $100 first prize.

We were all talking so much that none of us noticed Lyle Haywood, staring at the totem pole, his eyes transfixed, his mouth open.

"That's it," he whispered. *"I can't believe it! That's it! THAT'S IT!"*

2

We looked at Lyle, then the totem pole, then back to Lyle.

"What's 'it'?" I asked.

"The totem pole!" Lyle exclaimed. "Mrs. Peterson! How long have you had that totem pole?"

Mrs. Peterson was cooking in the kitchen, and she poked her head out the order window. She looked up, deep in thought. "The previous owner bought it at a garage sale a long, long time ago. It's been here since I bought the place, and it hasn't moved an inch in ten years. The thing is so heavy that it's hard to budge."

"I think I know why," Lyle said with a nod.

"What's the big deal?" Tony said. "It's an old totem pole."

"Guys, it's a lot more than that. Take a close look."

There were different kinds of faces, human and animal, that were carved into the totem pole. At the top was a large, yellow and black carved bumblebee.

It was Dylan who realized it first, and when he did, he about fell right out of his chair.

"Th . . . th . . . that's . . . that's it!" he stammered. "Lyle! You're right!"

"What?" Holly said. "What are you guys talking about?"

"Don't you see the faces?" Lyle said. "Start at the bottom. Tell me what you see."

Holly turned and looked at the totem pole. "I see a bear, a face, then another face of some sort, and a giant bumblebee at the top."

Shane leapt out of his seat. "You're right! That's it!"

"Bear, Face, Face, bee!" Lyle cried. "That's what was written on that note we found in the briefcase!"

I was so excited I knocked over my orange juice. Even Mrs. Peterson came to our table to see what all of the fuss was about.

"Mrs. Peterson . . . would you mind if we leaned your

totem pole over and laid it on the floor?"

"What on earth for?" she asked.

"There might just be something inside of it," Shane said. "Can we? We'll be real careful."

"Sure," Mrs. Peterson said. "Just stand it back up when you're finished."

We had to move a couple tables out of our way. Carefully . . . *very* carefully . . . the six of us leaned the totem pole over. A couple of other customers watched us, probably wondering what on earth we were doing.

Lyle gasped. "There's a plug in the bottom! The totem pole is hollow, and somebody plugged it up!"

"I'll bet it's not hollow," Holly said. "I'll bet that it's filled—"

"With silver dollars!" Dylan exclaimed.

Shane pulled out his pocket knife and handed it to Lyle. "Now," he said, "let's pull that plug out! "

3

Lyle used the blade of the knife to pry the plug out. He had to work at it for a few minutes. Finally, the plug fell to the floor. It was made of cork.. Dollar saw it and began batting it around in his paws.

"Okay, guys," Lyle said. "Lift the other end."

Dylan, Shane and Tony reached their arms around the top of the totem pole and lifted it up.

Instantly, coins began falling from the hole in the bottom!

"Silver dollars!" Holly exclaimed as the shiny discs rolled about on the floor.

"We found it!" Dylan cried, jumping up and down.

"We found the stolen loot! We found the stolen loot!"

The coins kept coming and coming. Shane, Dylan and Tony kept raising the top of the totem pole. Finally, when the totem was nearly straight up in the air, the coins stopped coming out.

"It's a lot lighter without all those dollars in there," Shane said. They righted the totem pole and it stood by itself.

There were silver dollars—dozens of them—scattered all over the floor. We all fell to our knees and began gathering them up like mad squirrels.

"They look almost brand new," I said, holding one of the silver dollars up. "They're still shiny."

We stacked the dollars in stacks of ten on the table. All in all, we counted one hundred thirteen silver dollars.

Mrs. Peterson was dumbfounded. She picked up a silver dollar. "And they've been right here, all along," she said, shaking her head.

"I'll bet that the totem pole was up in that old shed," Lyle said. "The robbers found out that it was hollow, and that's where they hid the money."

"And they put that note in the suitcase, so when they came back, they'd remember where they hid the dough!" Dylan exclaimed.

"Right on!" Shane said. "But they were killed in the shootout with police. Nobody knew that the totem pole was filled with the silver dollars, and it was probably sold by someone who had no idea what was inside."

It was incredible. Seeing all of those dollars there, shining like new, knowing that each one was worth a lot more than a dollar.

"So, if each one is worth around twenty dollars," Lyle said, and there are one hundred and thirteen coins, that means that the whole kit and kaboodle is worth—"

"—Two thousand two hundred and sixty dollars," Holly finished. She'd figured it out in her head, without using a calculator or anything.

All we could do was stare. I've never seen so much money in one place. None of us had.

And so, for the second time in one week, the Adventure Club made the papers. Norm Beeblemeyer did another article on us, and how we had found the missing money. He took a picture of the six of us standing around the piles of silver dollars, and he wrote an article about how we'd found them. Mrs. Peterson told us that since we were the ones who found the coins, we could have them. Shane called a coin shop in another town to see if he wanted to buy the coins, and he said that he'd pay eighteen dollars for each coin. That would be a total of two thousand and thirty nine dollars! That would mean three hundred thirty nine dollars for each of us!

We all felt like we were on the top of the world, and we all dreamed about what we were going to buy with our money.

But Holly received a phone call that changed everything.

4

I had just finished eating lunch when Holly came to the door.

"Have you got a minute?" she asked.

"Sure," I said. "What's up?"

"I just got a call from the director of the Great Bear Heart Historical Museum," she said. "She's interested in the silver dollars."

"Is that the lady that bought the slot machine?" I asked.

Holly nodded. "Yeah, that's her. And she wants the silver dollars for the museum. She said that they are a part of the town's history."

"How much did she offer you?" I asked.

Again, Holly shook her head. "Nothing," she replied. "She said that they don't have any more money, and she wondered if we would donate the silver dollars to the historical museum for free."

"For free?!?!" I gasped.

"That's what she said. She asked if we would think it over."

"What did you tell her?"

Holly shrugged. "I told her that I would tell everyone and we'd have to think about it."

So we called a special meeting of the Adventure Club, and met later in the day. We were in our new clubhouse, gathered in a circle on our milk crates as Holly explained. When she was finished, no one said anything.

Finally, after a few moments of silence, Tony raised his hand. "I vote we sell the coins to that coin collector and we split the money," he said.

No one raised their hands. Dylan started to raise his, but he lowered it when he saw that he was the only one.

"It's not that simple," Holly said. "The director said that those coins are a big part of our town's history, and she's right."

"But we found them!" Dylan exclaimed. "We found

them, and they're ours!"

"You're right," Holly said. "We found them, and Mrs. Peterson said we could have them. But she also said that it would be nice if we donated them to the museum."

"She knows that the museum wants the coins?" Shane asked.

Holly nodded. "I told her. I asked her what she thought we should do."

Well, the six of us got into one *big* argument. I stayed out of it and didn't say much, because part of me wanted my share of the money. But another part of me said that the coins really *did* belong in a museum where people could learn about the history of the town. I was really confused. Everybody else was, too. It seemed like we were all mad at each other. We couldn't agree on anything. Tony was shouting at Holly. Holly was shouting back. Even Dylan was yelling. Without any doubt, it was the worst argument that we'd ever had in the history of our club.

Finally, I spoke up. I had to yell to get everybody to quiet down. "Okay! Okay!" I said. "Here's what we do." Holly, Shane, Dylan, Lyle, and Tony looked at me. "We can split up the silver dollars among the six of us.

That would give us—" I paused and looked up into space as I tried to do the math in my head. Holly was faster.

"Eighteen coins each," she said, "and five left over."

"If we do that," I continued, "we can each decide what we want to do with our coins."

"Good idea," Tony said, giving the 'thumbs up' sign with both hands.

"Maybe we can donate the five remaining dollars to the museum," Dylan said. "Maybe that would make them happy."

There was another period of silence, and then Holly spoke.

"If we split the coins among us, I'm going to donate my share to the museum," she said flatly.

"You're crazy," Tony said bitterly.

"Maybe," Holly said. "But look at us. We're all fighting . . . over what?"

"Silver dollars," Lyle said.

"A lot of money," Tony offered.

"A *ton* of money," Dylan said.

"Yeah," Holly said, looking at each one of us. "And we're *fighting* about it. We're supposed to be friends."

"We *are* friends," Shane insisted.

"Until it comes to money," Holly said. "Look at us. We're fighting and arguing about *money?*"

"Fine with me," Tony said, crossing his arms defiantly. "It's a *lot* of money."

"Fine with me, too," Dylan agreed. "I've never had so much money. I'm going to be rich!"

"You guys go ahead and be rich," Holly said in disgust. She stood up, and I could see tears in her eyes. "You can keep my eighteen coins. I don't want them." She walked over to the trap door, opened it, and began climbing down the rope ladder. Before she disappeared, she turned and looked at us. Her expression was a mix of sorrow, anger, and hurt. Her eyes were glassy.

"You guys have always been my best friends," she said. "I've *always* thought that I was rich."

And with that, she climbed down the rope ladder, and vanished.

5

Wow. It sure is strange how things change when you sit back and think about them.

"She's just mad because she didn't get her way," Tony said. "She'll get over it."

There was a moment of silence, and then Shane shook his head. "She's right, you know."

"About what?" Dylan asked.

"Here we are arguing and fighting about something that really is kind of stupid," Shane replied. "Holly was just trying to do something nice."

"By giving the museum all of our silver dollars?!?!" Tony exclaimed.

Shane looked at Tony. "The director gave us a hundred dollars for that slot machine, remember?" he said. "That was pretty nice of her. Mrs. Peterson gave us the coins because we had found them. She said she knew we had been searching for them, and she thought we deserved them. Do you think the museum director or Mrs. Peterson are worried about being rich? Or, maybe, do you think they realize that some things are more important than money?"

"Like friends," I said quietly.

Tony hung his head, and we all were silent. The only thing we could hear was the gentle whisper of the wind moving through our giant maple.

"I don't know what to do," Shane said with a shrug. "We found the silver dollars, and now they belong to us. We could sell them to that collector for a lot of money. But, on the other hand, Holly is right. If we gave the coins to the Great Bear Heart Historical Museum, people from all over could learn more about the history of our town. They'd be able to see a part of the town's history in those coins."

"But we're always broke," Lyle said. "It seems like we get all of these great ideas, but we never have enough money to do anything."

"Such as . . . ?" Shane said.

Lyle said nothing.

"Think about it, guys," Shane continued. "We've always been able to get by. Really. We've always been able to do what we want, and when we didn't have the money to do something, we figured out a way around it. Or we figured out a way to make the money. We've always dreamed of having tons of money, because of all the cool things we could do."

"Now it seems to be more trouble than it's worth," Lyle said.

"Yeah, but . . . ." Dylan began, but he didn't finish.

And so, we talked about it, and we decided that the only thing we could do was divvy up the coins between us. That way, each of us could do what we wanted with our share. It was only fair.

"Don't forget," I said. "Holly has her share coming to her. I think she's mad, and I don't think she's going to come to the clubhouse to get her coins. I motion that we all go to her house in the morning."

Dylan raised his hand. "I second that," he said, and Tony, Lyle, and Shane agreed. We would all meet at the park in the morning, and then go to Holly's house. We were going to give her her share of the coins. Whatever she decided to do with them would be up to her.

It's not what Holly wanted, but as a club, we had voted on it, and we ruled against her. We voted to divide up the coins, and, to be fair, Holly had to accept her share.

I had a really hard time sleeping that night. My stomach was twisted in knots. I really hoped that Holly would understand. I hoped that she would understand, and she wouldn't be mad at us and quit the club.

Most importantly, I hoped she would still be my friend.

6

We met at the park at nine in the morning. Even Dylan was on time. Lyle and Shane carried the silver dollars, which we had put in a wooden box that Lyle's dad had. We made six piles of eighteen coins, which left five coins. The night before, we had decided for certain that we would give those five coins to the museum.

"Okay," Shane said, staring at the stacks of coins on the picnic table. "We all know what we have to do."

"Let's go," I said.

We walked up the hill. Tony and Shane carried the wooden box that contained Holly's share of the coins, and we arrived at her house a few minutes later. Dylan rang the doorbell, and Holly's mom came to the door.

"Yes, Holly is home," Mrs. O'Mara said. Then, she leaned forward and spoke quietly. "She's been upset about something, but I don't know what it is. Do you kids have any idea?"

"Well . . . maybe," I said.

"Yeah, maybe we can cheer her up," said Dylan.

Mrs. O'Mara disappeared, and after a moment, Holly came to the door. She said nothing.

"We voted to divvy up the silver dollars," Tony said. "We brought your share."

Tony and Shane placed the wooden box on the porch. "That's your portion," Lyle said.

"I told you guys I didn't want any part of it," Holly said. I could tell by her voice that she was still very upset.

"We know," Shane said. "But you know the rules. You've been a part of this club since the beginning."

"Not anymore," Holly said, shaking her head.

"Everybody makes mistakes, Holly," I said.

"Well, you can take my share of the coins and do what you want with them," she snapped. She looked very hurt.

"Fine," Shane said. "But you have to give them to us. If that's the way you want to be, then you have to open up the box and give us your share. Otherwise, we're going to leave them right here on the porch."

"Whatever," Holly said, and she knelt down and opened the wooden box. She threw the lid open and was about to grab the coins . . . then she froze.

"What in the—"

She stopped speaking and gazed into the box, looking at her share of the silver dollars.

All one hundred and thirteen of them.

7

Here's what we had done:

After we'd divided up the coins at the park, we each took our share and placed them back in the box. The night before, we had decided that Holly was right. Sure, it would be nice to have a lot of money. We all wanted our share of the silver dollars. Who wouldn't?

But our friendship was a lot more valuable.

When Holly saw all of the coins in the box, she was speechless. She just stared blankly at all of the silver dollars that glittered back at her from the wooden box.

"But . . . what . . . how . . . ?"

"We thought about it a lot after you left yesterday,"

Lyle said. "And you're right. We already *are* rich. All of us. We don't need any money to prove that."

"Besides," Dylan Bunker said softly. He was staring at the ground. I think he had a hard time speaking. "You're worth more than my share of the silver dollars, Holly," he mumbled.

"Yeah," I agreed. "Mine, too."

Lyle, Shane and Tony nodded.

Holly beamed, her eyes moist with tears. I will never forget the look in her eyes and the smile on her face. We were all friends once again. No amount of money in the world was going to split up the Adventure Club. We had just proven it.

All of the silver dollars now belonged to Holly, and she donated all of them to the Great Bear Heart historical museum.

And so, the mystery of the stolen silver dollars was solved. Now people who visit the Great Bear Heart Historical Museum can actually see the coins up close. Plus, the old totem pole is still at *The Kona* café, and people still use it to hang up their coats. We were still broke, of course, but none of us really complained. The *Independence* was in the Haywood's boathouse, and we planned to take her out again real soon. We had a new clubhouse. Our trip to the Grand Hotel on Mackinac Island had been really creepy . . . but it also was a lot of fun. And a forest fire had not only threatened the town, but our very lives . . . and we lived to tell about it.

And we learned that our friendship was more important than any amount of money in the world. I've heard a saying that says 'the best things in life are free'.

Don't believe it for a minute.

Believe this:

The best things in life . . . aren't *things*.

Summer ended and school started. I like school, but I have to admit that I really was sad to see the summer go. We'd had so much fun and so many cool adventures. There was no way that we'd ever have so much fun again.

That's what I thought, anyway.

Until one day when Shane Mitchell called an emergency meeting of the Adventure Club. He wouldn't say why, but he said that it had to do with the old, abandoned schoolhouse over on Walker Street There have always been a lot of rumors about the place. Over the years, lots of people have said they've seen strange things in and around the old, boarded-up school.

And when we held a meeting and decided that the

Adventure Club should investigate, we had no idea what we were getting ourselves into. We'd always considered the schoolhouse 'off limits', since it was so old and spooky.

Not anymore.

Now, we were going to investigate, and find out once and for all if the old schoolhouse really *was* haunted.

And, as you can imagine, it would lead to an adventure that we would never forget . . . .